AF429103

# WENDY ASHFORD

# The GRUMP and the CHEF

# Want to get more news from Wendy?

Sign up for the author's New Releases mailing list
and be the first to know when a new book comes out!
You will periodically receive news and offers.

Follow this link to get started:
https://wendyashford.com/newsletter/

To all the grumps out there,
you are my favorite companions.

# Chapter 1

"Greg is going to propose." I glance at Ava in line next to me at the cafe as we're getting ready to order our lattes.

She arches a perfect chestnut brow, studies me for an endless moment, and then wrinkles her nose. It's not the reaction I was hoping for from my best friend.

"What makes you think that?" Her expression is suspicious.

"He was edgy when we met my father for lunch on Sunday. He probably asked him for permission." I can't contain my excitement.

We've been living together for three years now, dating for five. It's the next natural step for a couple that's been in a relationship this long. I can't wait to hire a wedding planner and dive into this new adventure.

"Greg is always on pins and needles when he meets your father. That man is scary," she says while giving the barista our orders.

We move out of the way and watch the usual Wednesday morning crowd in Manhattan. It's a perfect mix of professionals and tourists, giving this city the unique vibe it's famous for.

"He is not. He just wants the best for his daughter," I counter.

She raises her eyebrow again, calling out my bull-shit.

"Okay, I admit he is kind of intimidating, but he'd never hurt anyone," I agree.

We grab our cups and walk out of the crowded cafe. I close my eyes, taking in the sun and the aroma of coffee while I take a sip. It's an end-of-October cold day. Soon, we'll be facing rainy days and freezing temperatures, but also Christmas decorations, and I'm here for all of it.

"Why are you so excited? You're not thinking about marrying him, right?" She glances at me while sipping her coffee.

Again, not the face I expected from her. It's her habit to hide behind her drink when she doesn't want me to know what's on her mind. A bit of my enthusiasm slips away.

"Why shouldn't I? We live together. Nothing major will change from that point of view." My voice comes out insecure. My life with Greg isn't a rollercoaster of excitement, but it's not that bad.

Wendy Ashford—The grump and the chef

She grabs my hand and stops me in front of the glass door of the *Taste and Dream* sign. Our offices are only a few floors up from here. "I'm not saying the news isn't exciting, but are you sure you want to tie the knot with him? You basically forced him into living together." She smiles, trying to reassure me, but the hole in the pit of my stomach doesn't get any smaller.

"My lease was ending, and it was stupid to pay two rents in a city like New York." I try to justify something we've been discussing for three years. She thinks Greg didn't want to move in with me because he didn't ask to. But he would have said no if he didn't want to, right?

"You've been a couple for five years—how often have you met his parents?" She asks to prove her point.

"They live in Florida!"

"Okay. During all these years, you never had time to catch a plane and fly there?" She raises an eyebrow.

She's never liked him. She's always thought he's only with me because it's safe. *I'm* safe. With a dependable, good job. I tend to plan without setting unrealistic expectations, don't rush decisions, and am reliable. She thinks I chose him because he was the first man to ask me out for more than a month. I've never had a steady boyfriend before. Each one of the guys I dated got bored after a while, so when he kept asking me out, I thought he was *The One*.

Ava always tells me that life with a man, *my* man, is expected to be exciting. I should feel fluttery wings in my stomach every time I see him. I don't see it this way. Life with the right person have to be solid and reliable, not like my parents, who got divorced and remarried God only knows how many times. Butterflies are for teenagers, and I'm a twenty-seven-year-old woman who need to think about a family, not a juvenile crush.

"Why can't you be excited for me?" I pout.

She glances at me and grins, a sincere one this time. "Look, if you're thrilled, I'm happy for you." She kisses me on the cheek.

I smile back. I don't seek her approval, but I want to share this happiness with my best friend.

"And my brother is the greatest divorce lawyer I know. We will kick Greg's ass!" she adds, laughing.

"Ava!" I swat her arm as we enter our building and stroll toward the elevators, chuckling because she always has my back.

***

"Olivia, can you come to my office, please?" I shift my gaze away from the computer to peer at Greg standing at the door.

He leans against the doorjamb, his tousled blond curls falling over his forehead. He's wearing his gray suit today, and I can't stop checking him out.

12

When I first came to work here, I thought he was handsome, but then I discovered he was smart too. He's the chief editor of the publishing house, and while company policy forbids relationships between colleagues, it says nothing about marriages.

We've been dating since I was a junior editor, and inside this place, we keep our relationship strictly professional to avoid arousing suspicion. Which is why it's a bit surprising he came all the way down here to demand that I go to his office two floors up.

"Yes, sure." Standing up, I follow him out toward the elevator. When I march by Ava's cubicle, she looks at me with a questioning expression. Shrugging my shoulders, I shake my head in response.

The ride up to his floor is silent and tense. A million thoughts cross my mind, and I even contemplate the idea that he's about to ask me to marry him. It's not my ideal choice for a romantic setup for going down on his knee, but who am I to complain? A proposal is a proposal, no matter where it happens. I always thought the gesture has more meaning if you don't plan it out in detail. Maybe Greg decided to do something impulsive and chose not to wait for a vacation or a dinner out.

We slip into his office without a word while some colleagues peer curiously at us. When he closes the door, I realize we won't have much privacy, considering the glass walls separating us from the rest of the open space. I hope he doesn't get into trouble for what he's about to do, but we should be fine as long he doesn't kneel in front of me.

He gestures toward the chair opposite his desk, and I take a seat. Uptight is an understatement for how I'm feeling. Greg sits down across from me and pulls a file-sized container from the floor behind him. I'm a bit taken aback. I mean, I hoped there was a box involved, but not something this big.

Frowning, I study him. He's nervous, but at this point, I don't know why.

"Olivia, I hate to be the one to tell you this, but we have to let you go." His voice is quiet and sweet.

I stare at him without grasping the meaning of what he is saying. "Sorry, what?" I blurt out after what seems an eternity.

"We've been having some problems lately and we need to cut costs. It saddens me, but considering our affair, I think it's best for you to pursue your career elsewhere."

My frown deepens. This is a joke, right? "Is it because we're getting married? Is it against company policy?"

It's his turn to scowl and search my face for an explanation. "Marry you? No. I'm reevaluating our relationship, and I don't think we should work together. HR asked me to reduce some expenses, and I thought this would be the most desirable solution for both. I don't think you want to see me daily once we break up. I'm doing you a favor and letting you go."

I open my mouth, trying to come up with a sharp reply, but I'm so dumbfounded the only thing I can manage to squeal is: "Are you dumping me?"

Greg folds his hands on his desk and nods. "Well, yeah…"

"You're firing me because you're dumping me?" I ask, shocked.

He frowns and shakes his head. "No, I'm laying you off because we're cutting costs *and* I'm doing you a favor. I mean, you'd be crying every time you see me, and that would be embarrassing for you. I care about you, and I don't want to make this even more difficult."

I honestly don't feel the need to cry in front of him. No. I want to punch him in the face. How dare he dump me *and* fire me? Or fire me and dump me—I'm not even sure which one came first.

"Are you trying to make this easier for me or for you, Greg?" I ask indignantly.

"I'm okay. Thanks for asking."

Is he for real? "So, that's it? After five years, you're ditching me like an old shoe? And here I was thinking you were tense because you were going to ask me to marry you—how stupid can I be!" I blurt out with an incredulous laugh.

He glances over my shoulder, maybe because I raised my voice and he's worried I'll cause a scene. "Olivia, let's be honest. It wasn't working between us. Don't you agree?" He speaks in a condescending tone like I'm a child and I can't grasp the meaning of what he is saying.

"I thought you were going to propose, so no, *Greg*, I thought everything was fine," I bark.

He nails me to the chair with a disapproving glance. What did he expect? That I would just accept this without a word? Looking at him now, I realize it's exactly like that. I think back to what Ava always says about us, about our relationship. Am I that quiet and predictable that I would agree to something like this and not cause a scene? Apparently, Greg thinks so.

"I'll stay with a friend for a few days so you can move out of the apartment without having me there," he explains, and I get the idea he's been planning this for quite a while now.

"How considerate of you." My words drip sarcasm.

"I know, but I told you. I care about you, and I want to make it smooth for you."

I'm baffled. Speechless. Completely shocked. Did I really spend five years of my life with this manipulator?

"You know what? I'm going to make it easy for you too. Give me that file box, and I'll leave my office right now," I say in a sweet tone.

He smiles. He has the nerve to smile at me as if nothing happened in this room. "I knew you'd understand."

Yes, because I'm the one who always understands, right Greg? I grab the container and go back to my desk.

16

"What did he want?" Ava asks. She made an effort to wait fifteen minutes to satisfy her curiosity before entering my cubicle and closing the door behind her.

"Oh, nothing. He dumped and fired me. Or fired and dumped me. I didn't quite understand the sequence." Anger drips from every word.

She gasps and sits in the chair in front of my desk. "He did not!"

"Oh yes, he did. Now I know why he was so anxious." I start putting my notepads into the box he gave me. After six years working for this company, I have a lot to remove.

"Are you suing him? I mean, you can totally sue his ass. I can ask my brother if he has a colleague who could do it," she suggests, and I smile at her.

After everything that's just happened, what bothers me most is that I wasted years of my life working for him here. I was young, I needed a job. I accepted this one because it paid well and it was somewhat related to what I like to do: cooking. But I never loved it. Now that I think about it, I don't even feel sad that he broke up with me. How messed up is that?

"I'm not wasting any more time on him. I'm done and out of here."

She frowns and peers at me, puzzled. "So, no revenge?" she pouts.

A small laugh escapes my lips. "Oh, no. I already took care of that. Do you remember the three books I was editing for a Christmas release that have a deadline next week? Well, I just deleted all my edits. They're virgins, just like they arrived five months ago. Good luck fixing that, Greg."

A wicked smile spreads on her face. "I love the sound of this! I'll try to film his reaction and send you a video when he finds out."

"Wait until I go back to his apartment to grab some of my stuff and accidentally spill bleach on all his suits," I smirk, tasting my payback almost physically on my tongue.

Ava whimpers. "Why do you have to retaliate on all those beautiful, tailored perfections?"

I raise a brow and cross my arms over my chest. "He just ditched me and fired me. He's lucky I'm not dragging him to court!"

She inhales. "That is always the best solution. You know you would win, right?"

I look at my box and my heart sinks into my stomach. "I know. But I don't want to drag this story out, prolonging my humiliation. I thought he was going to pop the question, and he dumped my ass. How humiliating is that? How stupid was I?"

Ava smiles sweetly at me, making me feel like a child who's failed miserably. "Don't even think like that. He's the asshole manipulative one. It's not your fault."

"Yeah," I nod, but I don't feel any better.

"So? Are you going to stay with me for a while?"

Wendy Ashford—The grump and the chef

I shake my head. "Nope. I need to regroup, think about what I want to do with my life, find a new job, a new apartment. There's only one place far enough away where I can do that," I say with renewed conviction.

"No! You can't abandon me during this season. There's Halloween, Thanksgiving, and Christmas. What will I do if you fly to the soaked Pacific Northwest?" she complains.

I laugh. She's such a drama queen. "First, you're in Manhattan. There are plenty of people you can hang out with. Second, I'll only stay for a couple of weeks. I'll be back before the festivities start. I'm not abandoning you."

Ava sulks but knows that when I'm overwhelmed with something life throws at me, the only place where I can calm down and think is in the middle of nowhere on the Olympic Peninsula.

# Chapter 2

"Do you have more dog food?" I ask Henry, who is watching something on his phone behind the counter.

He peeks at me with a smile. "A couple more in the back; is that enough?"

"Yes, sure. Should be okay," I answer, eyeing the three huge bags I'll use to feed Jack I already have in my cart.

I check my list one last time to be certain I didn't forget anything. The snow is coming early this year, and I won't be able to come to town for a while for supplies I may have forgotten.

"Do you have everything you need?"

Glancing back at the man, I notice his worried face. He's in his sixties and has been running this grocery store in the middle of nowhere since he was eighteen, taking over after his father's death. This place has been in his family for generations, like every other business in this borough of six hundred souls.

Each year it's the same story: I come here to buy provisions to survive the cold season isolated up in the mountains, and he tries to convince me to accept a job in town because it's safer than where I reside. Like always, I'm prepared to decline his invitation.

"Yes, this is the last trip before winter," I mumble without looking him in the eyes. While I sometimes appreciate talking to someone besides Jack, the mixed German shepherd and border collie I live with, I always find it difficult to tell him no.

"You know my offer to work here still stands, right? I need a strong guy like you to help me stock deliveries in the back." His suggestion is tentative. After years of refusing to be employed here, he already knows what my answer will be, but it doesn't stop him from asking.

"I have animals up there. I can't abandon them to come down here during the colder weather." My voice is firm.

He smiles and shakes his head as he scans my provisions on the cash register. "You have a chicken coop and a dog. You can bring them here. All you need is a garage to keep them from freezing to death," he points out, and I feel embarrassed. My excuse is not solid, but I'm tired of trying to make him understand that I'm good where I am. Alone and without neighbors for miles.

"You have a teenager helping you out with the store. You'd have to fire him," I add with a smile.

Henry sighs, looking almost exasperated. "God, I would do him a favor. He's counting the days until he goes to college and disappears from this town. He's always playing videos on his phone."

"You were watching a video on your cell too." I smirk at him.

The grin that appears on his face is priceless. He grabs the device from his pocket and shows me the recording of a toddler trying to get up and walk. "This is my grandkid, Sophia. Those are her first steps. Before too long, she'll be driving my wife crazy running around the house." He beams proudly.

A pang hits my chest seeing the tentative pace of the kid. A downside of living alone up in the mountains is that I'll never have kids running all over the house or achieving their milestones. That train left the station a long time ago, and I'm not delusional enough to hope it will ever come back.

"She's adorable." My voice cracks a bit around the knot in my throat.

"She really is. Oh, by the way, it almost slipped my mind. My wife told me to give you something to read. She said you'll love these." He grabs a box from behind him and hands it to me. There are at least twenty books here.

"Thank her. I'll bring them back this spring, I promise." I smile at him.

Wendy Ashford—The grump and the chef

"Please, don't. We're drowning in novels, and we don't have any more room for them. But she keeps buying them. I tried to convince her to buy one of those big phones where she can read all she wants, but she said it's not the same as leafing through the pages."

A chuckle escapes my lips as I imagine Marla making a fuss about all the technology she hates. Or at least some of it; she's not complaining about online orders and the delivery of her paperbacks.

I leave Henry to his videos, grab a few sacks of dog food from the back, and start loading my pickup. My gaze goes up to the gray sky. The weather forecast says it will be snowing for the next week, kicking off the early snow season. Last year, we had almost thirty feet of it from November to May. I hope we don't reach that record again. I'll be stuck inside until June.

Breathing deeply, I take in the smell of pine that gives its name to this town, Pinecreek. The biggest and only street is surrounded by majestic pine trees, and the houses nestled in between them resemble a gnome village. No matter how isolated this place is, I love the peace of the trees and snow here.

After loading my truck, I cover the cartons with a tarp and stroll a few feet to the only pub around. There's no one in here except Mia, the bartender working this shift.

"It's quiet tonight." I catch her attention as I sit on a stool in front of her.

She turns her gaze from the TV over the bar and smiles when her eyes rest on me. She tilts her head and studies me for a while. She is around my age, thirty-two, born and raised in this area, not far from where she works. She got married in her twenties, divorced a couple of years later, and never popped a child out as most of the women she grew up with.

"They're all getting ready for the storm," she explains, grabbing a glass, pouring my favorite beer, and giving it to me. I sip the cold drink and sigh in relief. Damn, I will miss this for the next few months.

"Shouldn't you be getting ready?" I raise my brow at her.

She chuckles and uses a rag to clean a few drops of beer that spilled onto the wooden surface. "Living upstairs, I don't have to step one foot outside to get here. Just have to unlock the doors over there and wait for the snowplow to clean the streets." She points to the wooden door behind me.

"Fair enough."

"What can I bring you? Burger and fries as usual?" she asks leaning on the counter and winking seductively.

She's a beautiful woman with jet-black hair and sleeve tattoos that give her a badass air. She's asked me out a couple of times, or better yet, to have some fun before I isolate myself for the season, but I always found an excuse not to have sex with her.

Wendy Ashford—The grump and the chef

When I need to "take care of my needs" as she says, I prefer to go out of town when the weather allows it. This place is microscopic, everyone knows each other. I don't want to stir up a fuss fucking someone I know and then dumping her because I don't feel like having a relationship.

"Double fries, please!" I plead.

She chuckles before walking to the kitchen to set up my order. When she comes back, she brings two plates, one for the burger and one for the hugest portion of fries I have ever seen.

I laugh and dive straight into the potato mound. "You know how to make a man happy."

She scrutinizes me with humor in her eyes. "I know other ways to make a man happy, but I'm not asking you again. There is a limit to how many times a girl can bear to be turned down."

I glance sheepishly at her, not wanting to hurt her feelings. This is why I avoid fucking her, even if she is gorgeous.

"You know how I feel about doing it casually." I bite into my dinner and almost moan. I will crave this more than I want to.

"Not every woman wants a relationship, Noah," she insists.

I shrug my shoulders and swallow the bite with a sip of beer. "You all say that, but then you want more,

The grump and the chef—Wendy Ashford

and when a man gives you what you want, you change your mind," I mumble a bit harshly.

She crosses her arms over her chest and peers at me curiously. "Stop thinking that everyone is like your ex," she remarks before turning around and strutting toward the kitchen.

What I thought was my last decent meal until spring ends up leaving a sour taste in my mouth. I'm tempted to follow her into the back and apologize, but I know that one apology leads to other arguments, and I'd find myself dodging her proposals.

There's a reason why I never found another woman: I don't want to deal with the consequences of physical attraction. I cannot handle seeing the other person again and trying to act casual. I have sex out of town mostly because I know I'll never see those women again.

I finish my dinner, leave the money next to my plate, and then head out, shouting a "Bye!" to Mia. She pops her head out of the kitchen just in time to see me disappear behind the door.

I amble to my pickup, secure the tarp covering my supplies, and hit the road. There's not a soul around tonight, and it takes me less than five minutes to reach the dirt path that leads to my cabin ten miles up the mountain. The best part of living here is that no one ventures up this road that looks more like a trail than something you can drive a car on.



Wendy Ashford—The grump and the chef

I park in the shelter attached to my cottage and un-load the supplies into the room in the back, where I stash food for the winter.

I check the chicken coop, refill the food and water, and then reach the front to close the barn doors with my truck inside to protect it from the icy temperatures.

I look up, and for an instant, I think I see a light in the woods. It's just a heartbeat, but I'm sure it's there, and then it's gone. I frown. The only structure around here is an old hut half a mile away that hunters use during spring and summer, but this time of year it's empty. I don't know if it's even inhabitable in winter—someone would freeze their ass off staying there.

I stare at the point for a few minutes, watching for another glimpse or flash of light, wondering if it was just my imagination. It's already pitch dark, and I don't want to venture over there to see if someone is crazy enough to come up here through a blizzard. Nothing. No more lights. I breathe in the frigid air and look up when I feel the first snowflakes hitting my skin.

I walk inside to the warmth of my cabin, and I'm welcomed by Jack, wagging his tail on the blanket in front of the fireplace. I scratch behind his ears and use a log to revive the embers. "Hey buddy," I greet him as I sit in the armchair next to the fire.

I close my eyes and enjoy the sound of the wood crackling, slowly consumed by the flame, and the forest preparing silently for the snowstorm.

# Chapter 3

"Mom! What do you mean *pinkish key ring?*" I ask as I turn off the car and stare at the hunter's cabin in front of me. "Mom!" I shout when no answer comes from the other side of the line.

Looking at my phone, I realize there is no reception up here. Great. I turn off the headlights and inhale before holding my breath. God, I should have stopped when I realized I'd grabbed the wrong keys from my mother's cabinet, the ones with GPS coordinates on the tag instead of a real address.

"Awesome!" I mumble, exasperated, leaning my forehead on the steering wheel. "Now I have to spend the night in the middle of the forest."

At least I rented a Jeep, so I'll be safe driving back to the main road tomorrow and looking for a hotel—if it exists. Pinecreek is not what you'd call a tourist attraction. I should have waited for my mother to give me the right key to the place instead of rummaging



Wendy Ashford—The grump and the chef

through her chaos looking for it myself. A pinkish key-ring, she said. What color is *pinkish*? And compared to what?

Her grandfather left two cabins for our family in this town. One cute little rustic place just outside Main Street that we stayed in sometimes when I was a kid for summer vacations, and this nightmare in front of me that she rents to hunters during spring and summer. Of course, I grabbed the nightmare keys!

I've always loved the Pacific Northwest because it reminds me of my childhood. When I feel over-whelmed by something in my life, I come here to re-charge. Until now, I've always come with someone like Ava or Greg, and I choose a more popular location, like Leavenworth or some other place around Seattle, for their sake. They're New Yorkers, they don't do well with dirt roads and moldy trees.

"Well, Olivia. Suck it up. You can't stay in your car or you'll freeze to death," I whisper to myself, but in the eerie silence of the forest during a snowy night, it sounds like a shout.

Turning on my seat, I grab my roller suitcase from the backseat and my purse from the front and drag them to the front door. A few snowflakes start to fall on my hands as I use my phone to light the keyhole and unlock the door. It opens with a creak into a one-room cabin that smells of dust and mold. The furniture, five pieces in total, is covered with white sheets. There's one small single bed against the far wall, a table and two chairs on the opposite side next to a stove and a small sink, and an armchair in front of the empty fireplace. No trace of a door leading to a bathroom.

"You have got to be kidding me."

Touching the wall next to the door, I grope for a light switch, but when I find it, my hopes are crushed—nothing happens when I turn it on.

"So, no lights, no bathroom, and no fireplace. Because there is no chance I can find wood and matches in the pitch dark." I rub a hand over my face trying not to cry.

What did I get myself into? I'm tempted to go back to town, but it's almost midnight, and the trail leading here was beyond challenging. I don't trust my driving skills to get back to town without having an accident. I'd be screwed for real if that happened.

I take a deep breath and immediately regret my decision when dust fills my lungs, making me cough. I close the door behind me, and the darkness is almost black, even though the one small window has no curtains.

"I can survive one night in here." My voice comes out firmer than I expected, and I realize it's comforting to speak out loud, even if no one can hear me.

Walking to the bed, I remove the sheet and find three thick blankets covering it. "Thank God. At least I won't freeze during the night."

Wendy Ashford—The grump and the chef

I start to take off my jacket but stop when I feel the cold. I open my suitcase, pull out my fleece unicorn jumpsuit and a pair of wool socks, and put everything on over my pants. I finish pulling up my jumpsuit while taking off my jacket, then put it on the bed and ball it up to use as a pillow.

"There, I should be fine." I smile, realizing I'm not cold anymore.

I lie down on the bed, grimacing and wondering if some animal has ever nestled in this mattress. I don't even want to know. I cover myself with the three blankets and close my eyes. The silence is almost surreal. I'm used to Manhattan, where there's something going on at all hours of the day and night. The Big Apple is never soundless unless you live in a penthouse on the top floor of a huge skyscraper, but that's definitely not me.

I don't know if this silence terrifies me or not. It would be worse if I heard a sound I don't recognize, right? That would mean there's something lurking in the dark room, and I do *not* want that! I try to slow down my racing heart and divert my thoughts elsewhere, reminding myself that tomorrow morning I'll go back to town, and everything will be fine.

With a pleasant surprise, I notice it's not pitch dark anymore the next time I open my eyes. Rubbing them, I sit up, grab my phone, and turn it on. Nine in the morning. I smile. It was easier than I thought. I fell asleep fast and never woke up. No nightmares and nothing walking on my face during the night.

I glance around and realize that this place, in the dim light, is less creepy than I thought. It's bare, without any nice, comfortable amenities, but it's just a shelter for hunters to crash for a night or two instead of camping. It's got more to offer than a tent.

I slip out of bed, put on my pink Uggs and my jacket, and head for the sink. At least I can wash my face before going back into town. I turn on the faucet, but just like the lights, nothing happens. I exhale, shaking my head.

"Are you kidding me?" I was just thinking this place wasn't complete crap, but I'm starting to reconsider my second impression. Maybe the water pipes froze because of the cold? I have no idea, but it's just another reason to get out of here as soon as possible.

I turn toward the only window next to the door and freeze on the spot. It's white. And not because there's a thin layer of snow outside—the window is literally blocked by a chalky wall. How much did it snow last night? I rush to the door and open it. Panic starts to rise in my chest when I find myself in front of a solid barricade. There is no way out of here, and there is absolutely no way I can drive back to town through this packed pile. I can't even see my Jeep out there!

"No. No. Nononononono!" I start to freak out. "Oh my God, I'm going to die here!"

Wendy Ashford—The grump and the chef

When the realization of what is happening settles in my chest, I go into full panic mode. I'm trapped in the middle of nowhere without food, water, heating, or a bathroom to relieve myself. They'll find my dead body this spring when it melts, preserved in the cold, soaked in my own excrement. How humiliating is that?

I feel the urge to scream, and I do. "Help! Somebody help me! I'm trapped here!" I shout until my throat hurts.

A few minutes pass and then a voice yells from the other side of the white wall, "I'm coming! Don't freak out, I'm coming."

Oh my God. I'm already hallucinating. I'm hearing voices. Is it the lack of oxygen? The snow has probably cut my air supply, sealing me inside this cabin, and I breathed it all last night while I was sleeping. No wonder I slept well, I was oxygen deprived. *Oh my God! Oh my God! Oh my God!*

"Help! Help me! I'm dying in here!" I shout louder than before, panic gripping my stomach.

"Shut up! I'm coming, and you're not dying!" The gruff voice from before shouts back.

I shut my mouth. Well, I could at least hallucinate someone nicer than this. I don't have time to reply before a spray of snow hits me, covering my entire face. I blink once, twice, trying to understand what is happening. A hand appears in the middle of the snow wall in front of me, then an arm, and at last, a face. A gorgeous, bearded face with two huge green eyes. God, this guy is breathtaking.

"Are you okay in there?" he asks, but it takes me a few seconds to understand he's talking to me. I'm staring at him like a stalker.

"Yes. How did you get here? Did you dig a tunnel from the road further down?" I ask, and I don't need to glance at his perplexed face to know it was a stupid question. Nobody digs a tunnel miles up the mountain to save someone they don't even know is there. There must be another explanation.

"No, I walked here from my house to check if there was someone here. I saw your car, and then I heard you shout," he explains in a deep voice.

God, can he be more manly? And to answer my silent question, he pushes away the remaining snow and stands before me in all his glory. He's about six feet two, his broad shoulders and narrow waist wrapped in a red plaid down jacket, brown cargo pants stretching over his massive thighs.

"So the snowfall didn't bury the entire cabin?" I ask in a shaky voice.

He tilts his head and frowns at me like I'm crazy. I wave my hands toward the white powdery wall covering the entire door, the one he just pushed down. When he realizes what I'm implying, he struggles to hide a smile.



Wendy Ashford—The grump and the chef

"No, the wind picked up in the direction of your front door and pushed the snow up alongside it, freezing it there. There's a little over a foot on the ground," he explains, and I realize that this makes more sense than six feet dumped on our heads in one night.

"Thank God! I can drive back to town," I mumble, relieved, pressing a hand over my racing heart.

The frown on his forehead deepens, and he studies me like I'm crazy. I'm starting to get annoyed at the way he glares at me. "You can't go back there. It's still snowing. The trail is completely covered and slippery. This snowstorm is going to last at least a week." He explains this to me like I'm a child who can't understand why she can't go to Disneyland.

"And what am I supposed to do? Stay here?" I blurt out, panic starting to creep into my stomach again.

He shakes his head.

"No, seriously, what should I do?" I insist when anxiety starts to grip my stomach.

"I don't know. Why are you here?" He's clearly puzzled by my presence, and I would be too if I were in his place.

"By mistake. I was supposed to grab the key for a cabin on Main Street, but I ended up here. I don't have food, water...not even a bathroom. How can I survive for a week in a snowstorm?" My voice is shaking. I want to cry. What the heck am I doing here and how can I get back?

He takes a deep breath and rubs a hand over his face like he's thinking about a solution. I don't even breathe while I wait for him to speak.

"Listen, come with me to my cabin. It's half a mile from here. You can crash on my couch until we figure out something, okay?" he proposes, but doesn't seem happy about it.

I cross my arms over my chest. "No way. You could be a serial killer for all I know." Why else would a guy like him live in a place like this? There's nothing here.

He stares at me like I'm a bug he has to deal with but doesn't want to. "I'm rescuing you! Why would I want to kill you?" he practically shouts.

"I don't know! There are a lot of crazy people around!" I shout back.

"I would have to bury your body somewhere. Do you know how hard it is to dig a hole in the frozen ground? It would be easier to just leave you here to starve to death," he points out, exasperated.

He's got a point. And I am starving, and I do need to pee. Badly. "Okay," I mumble, not knowing what else to say. I gaze around the cabin, not sure what to do. "Give me a second to grab my stuff."

He stares at me like he wants to say something but doesn't know where to start. "Are you wearing that?" he asks finally.

I look down and my cheeks burn with embarrassment. I forgot what I'd put on last night to go to bed. I

look ridiculous, but I won't give him the satisfaction of feeling uncomfortable in my own skin. I push my chin up, grab my suitcase, and meet him at the door.

"I'm ready," I say resolutely.

He shakes his head and rubs his eyes like he doesn't know what to do with me, then he turns around and starts to walk along what I'm guessing is the trail, covered in snow.

I close the door behind me and follow him.

It takes us forty-five freaking minutes to walk half a mile. The storm picks up as soon as we leave my cabin, and my Uggs get stuck in the snow a million times, so I have to dig them out every time. Fortunately, he figures out that we can walk much faster if he helps me with the suitcase and picks it up for me. It looks like a toy in his massive arms.

When we finally enter his cabin, I'm exhausted.

"The bathroom is over there." He points to a door at the back of the cozy place, and I don't think twice before running to it and taking off my clothes.

Before coming out again, I try to fix my crazy hair into a messy bun and wash my face. I grab a bit of his toothpaste and wash the disgusting taste out of my mouth. When I walk out, I'm at least somewhat presentable.

I find him putting some logs into the fireplace in a corner of the room, next to a comfortable-looking couch. I study his back, the massive shoulders and muscles darting under the thin fabric of his gray t-shirt. His naked arms are even bigger than they looked under his jacket. His hair is long and gathered on his head in a man bun—I hadn't noticed it under the beanie he was wearing when he rescued me. The more I take a good look at this guy, the more I'm drooling over him. Seriously, he is gorgeous.

As if feeling my gaze, he turns around and beckons me to sit on the couch. I glimpse around at the cabin on my way. This place is the definition of a log cabin. Everything is made of solid wood, with patches of plush carpet next to the full-size kitchen and in front of the dark gray couch. It's an open space with hardwood floors and a wooden staircase leading upstairs, where I assume his bedroom is located. It's manly but cozy at the same time.

"You should sit down. I'll make you something to eat," he orders in a gruff voice.

"Can I help? You don't have to do it yourself." I start to get up from the couch, but he pins me with a glare that makes me shiver.

He comes back a few minutes later with a cheese sandwich and a cup of coffee.

"So, you live here?" I ask when he doesn't seem to want to start a conversation.

"Yes."

Okay. He doesn't talk much. "Why?" The question is out of my mouth before I can think better of it.

Wendy Ashford—The grump and the chef

He stares at me but doesn't reply, so I bite on my cheese sandwich and moan. Literally moan when my tastebuds meet this rich, precious taste. Maybe it's because I haven't eaten anything since yesterday at the Seattle-Tacoma airport, but this sandwich is delicious. Sipping my hot coffee, I almost cry. An hour ago, I thought I was going to die. This must be heaven.

"So, seeing as how we're stuck here together for a few days, I'm Olivia." I extend my hand to introduce myself.

He lets out a sound between a laugh and a cough. "Days. More like weeks or months," he mumbles grumpily.

The blood drains from my face. "Sorry, what?" I must have misunderstood him. He can't possibly have said weeks or months.

"The storm will dump at least five feet of snow, if it even stops after this week, according to the weather forecast."

"Okay, one week. But I can go back when it's sunny, right?" My voice lacks any certainty.

"The temperature will drop, making everything icy and slippery. It'll be impossible to reach town with my pickup or your Jeep," he grumbles, annoyed.

"Well, I can walk!" I suggest. He can't be serious about me staying here for weeks, let alone months.

"Over ten miles? I suggest not if you don't want to freeze to death." He says it like it's the most obvious thing.

And maybe for him, it is, considering he lives here, but I'm from New York, for Pete's sake. Nothing ever closes in New York, not a business or a street. Not even during a natural disaster.

"So, what—you never go to town? What do you eat? How do you survive?" I start to panic again.

His frowns at me like I'm a kid bothering him with stupid questions. "I'm prepared to stay up here until spring."

Luckily, I'm sitting on this couch, or I'd faint. "Until spring?"

"Last year was even longer. I wasn't able to reach town until almost June." He observes me like he doesn't know if I'll freak out or not.

Not going to disappoint him. Of course, I'm freaking out. Is he crazy? "And what am I supposed to do? Stay here with you for months?" I squeal hysterically.

He shakes his head and raises his brow. "Well, sweetheart, you have no choice."

"Shit!"

Wendy Ashford—The grump and the chef

# Chapter 4

I study her face, even paler than before. Her blond hair is gathered over her head in a messy bun, making her wide hazel eyes stand out. Her pouty lips tremble at the realization that she's stranded with me for a while, like she wants to cry. I can't pinpoint if it's because she doesn't like me or because she has somewhere else to be, but either way, we're both screwed.

"It's not possible. I need to go back," she whines.

I stare at her and fold my arms over my chest, studying her while she checks out the bulge of muscle under my shirt. Olivia gawks at me like she's never seen a man before. I'd have to laugh if this wasn't such a shitty situation. Does she really think I want her here either? I live up this mountain because I hate being around people, especially curvy, five-foot-tall blondes that make my blood rush below the belt.

"Be my guest," I dare her, motioning toward the only exit.



The grump and the chef—Wendy Ashford

She glances at the door, then peeks at the storm raging outside the window and whimpers, hope dying in her eyes. I have no idea why she came here, but it's not my fault she's trapped in this mess.

"I need to go back for Thanksgiving. I promised Ava I would be back. How can I stay here for months? Are you sure we can't find a way to go down? I only need to reach the main road, then I can handle it from that point." Her voice cracks with emotion.

"Who do you think I am?" I reply with more anger than I intended. "I can't teleport you out of this place just because you want to. I don't care about how you're used to in New York, Princess, but you can't always get what you want."

She flinches at my rudeness, then rage replaces the emotion on her face. "How do you know where I'm from?"

Of all the things I said, that's what she picked up? "The tag on your suitcase has a Manhattan address," I clarify.

Her cheeks redden with embarrassment, but she pushes her stubborn chin high. She's a piece of work who's going to drive me nuts.

"Well, hermit-without-a-name, where I come from, we try to find a solution when we have a problem. We don't sit doing nothing because of a bit of snow," she spits angrily.

Wendy Ashford—The grump and the chef

She wants to intimidate me, but she looks like a cute little kitten with her fur all puffed out. A smile tugs at my lips, and I struggle to hide it.

"Well, Princess, do you have a solution?" I raise a challenging brow.

She glances at the storm outside, and the wind decides this is the perfect time to announce its presence, howling like a pack of hungry wolves. It can be scary sometimes, in particular at night. She shrinks into the cushions and exhales with a whimper.

Jack strolls into the living room, peeks at the new guest, jumps on the couch, and plops his head on her lap like he is friendly with her. She's startled but recovers in a heartbeat and scratches him behind his ears. He huffs, enjoying the cuddles.

"Traitor," I mumble under my breath, and I don't miss a smug smile appearing on Olivia's face. "My name is Noah, by the way, and this is Jack," I add.

"Well, nice to meet you, Jack. It's a pleasure to have someone happy about my presence in this house." She makes a show of not looking at me, her tone dripping with fake sweetness.

Picking up a book Marla gave me, I start to read. I'm too distracted by her presence to understand a single word of what I'm reading, but I don't glance in her direction. She sighs aloud, once, twice, three times in a span of a minute. In the end, I give up and glance at

her, and I find her staring at me while she scratches Jack's head.

"What?" I ask.

"What do you do when it snows?"

I raise the book in my hand in answer. She frowns.

"And?" Olivia goes on.

"And what?" I'm interested in her puzzled expression.

"You just read for months?" She appears shocked by the idea.

"Why not? It's snowing. What should I do?" Now I'm just messing with her.

"Don't you have a job?" Her curiosity is eating her alive.

"Not during the winter." I don't give up anything more. I like seeing her squirm.

"So, you read, and that's it? No TV or anything?" Her eyes are going to pop out of her sockets.

"No cable here, Princess. You'll miss your reality shows." This is a low blow even for my grumpy ass, but I don't like the expression on her face. She eyeballs me like I'm a different species altogether.

Olivia crosses her arms, gaining a disappointed huff from Jack. "I don't waste my time in front of reality shows, but I like to keep up with the real world by watching the news. You know? The world that keeps revolving out there while you hide your sorry ass up here," she spits indignantly.

44

I deserved that. I played the dumb blonde cliché card without knowing her. I don't make a habit of insulting people like that, but the idea of being stuck here with her for God knows how long is unnerving.

"Listen, the signal up here is shitty, and I don't have a TV. I have a computer I sometimes use with a satellite phone to download email with the most important news and the weather forecast, but it's expensive, and the internet is so slow I grow old looking at a web page. I'm aware of what's happening on this planet—major events like wars and elections reach this cabin. But I don't have entertainment. Okay?" I offer and observe her face relax, giving in to curiosity.

"So, you read a lot," she states, looking around, perhaps hopping to spot bookshelves.

"I have a Kindle, and I download a bunch of books during the summer when I go to town for work. Then I go through them in the winter when I'm forced to stay inside." I feel the urge to go into detail. I hope she's satisfied with my explanation and shuts up.

I lower my eyes to my book, and for a few minutes I flip through the pages in peace.

"Do you have any fantasy novels?" It's like she'll catch on fire if she keeps her mouth shut for more than a few minutes.

"No." I keep my eyes glued to the ink.

"So, what do you like?" She just doesn't stop babbling.

I grab the box Marla gave me and put it in front of her. She starts to browse the titles and wrinkles her nose. "The only guy I recognize is this one." She shows me Dave Grohl's biography.

"Good," I bring my eyes back to my book.

"He's the singer, right?" she asks cheerily.

"Among other things," I mumble.

"Do you like him?" She persists in talking.

"Yes," I exhale an exasperated breath. Does she ever shut up?

"Really?" Her astonished tone makes me peer at her.

I study her shocked face and frown, trying to understand if she's joking. "I grew up in the state where grunge was born. Of course, I like him!"

"You listen to grunge music? Like Nirvana?" She gapes at me like I'm from another planet.

I'm surprised she is informed about what grunge is and correctly associates it with Nirvana. I see lots of teenagers with Nirvana t-shirts, thinking it's a clothing brand.

"Yes, why is that so surprising?" I'm intrigued now.

"Don't know. Maybe it's your beard, man bun, or flannel jacket…you give me lumberjack vibes." She waves her hands around, pointing out my appearance.

"And lumberjacks don't listen to grunge music?" I ask, curious about where this conversation is going.

Wendy Ashford—The grump and the chef

"They give me more country, folkish vibes." She wrinkles her nose, shrinking shyly into the sofa. Maybe she realizes she's judging an entire category of people based just on their appearance. Precisely like I just did with the reality show comment. I'm sorry about that one.

"I'm from Washington State. I don't listen to country music!" I blurt out like she just insulted me.

She smiles sheepishly, and I go back to my book. Five minutes. The silence lasts a gargantuan five minutes.

"So, you don't have fantasy, huh?"

I huff, exasperated for the millionth time this morning, and put down my book. "No, I told you I don't have fantasy novels. Read something else." Growling at her sounds not so ridiculous.

Jack perks up his ears, picking up my discomfort. Scratching his belly, I hope he understands everything is okay. I don't need him acting skittish around her, considering I already have to deal with the most annoying woman in the world.

"But I don't like it," she pouts.

I rub a hand over my face, hoping it'll keep me from strangling her. "What can I do? Please, tell me what I need to do for you to keep your mouth shut for more than five minutes," I plead.

"Well, I have some fantasy novels I bought at the airport yesterday..." She tilts her head like I should understand what she is implying.

"And why aren't you reading them instead of bothering me?" I'm afraid of her answer.

"They're in the back seat of my Jeep," she whispers.

I stare at her. She's joking, right? Does she really think I'm going out in this weather to grab her books? She's crazy. "Well, too bad!" I go back to my biography until, from the corner of my eye, I see her stand up.

Olivia grabs her ridiculous unicorn jumpsuit, puts it on over her clothes, then layers up with another pair of socks, her useless pink Uggs, and finally, her jacket. She checks one last time that everything is buttoned up, and then she walks to the door.

"Where do you think you're going?" I ask, puzzled.

"To grab my books. In New York, we're used to solving our problems," she says, raising her chin stubbornly.

"Are you out of your mind? There's a snowstorm out there!"

"So what? We have snowstorms in the city too," she counters.

"And what do you do? Run around, dressed like a lunatic, in Central Park?" I struggle to hide my smile at the thought.

She doesn't answer but puts the hood of her jumpsuit, with a giant rainbow horn, on her head and goes out in the storm. I watch her through the window, struggling to walk against the strong wind and the snow slashing against her face. I give her five minutes

48

to realize it's an insane idea and come back with her tail between her legs.

Forty minutes later, I'm wearing my beanie, coat, and boots to go out and look for her. I'm worried I'll find her frozen and covered in ice. It'll be a bit challenging explaining to the sheriff why I have a dead woman in my pickup this spring.

I find her halfway to my place, entirely covered in frozen white crystals, with a massive paper bag in her arms. The snow is up to her knees, and she's struggling to keep her shoes on. I reach her, and without a word, scoop her in my arms, making her squeal in surprise. When I put her down on the carpet inside my cabin, her lips are blue, her teeth chattering loudly.

"Go take a shower and warm up while I will make lunch. Towels are on the cabinet under the sink."

I look at her as she tries and fails to smile, then grabs some clothes from her suitcase, her hands trembling from the cold. I shake my head while Jack wags his tail in front of the closed bathroom door.

"Don't get used to it. First chance she gets, she'll be running out of here to go back to the city." I learned something about women running from this place.

When she comes out, forty-five minutes later, she appears like another person. Her hair is damp and shiny, her cheeks are a healthy shade of pink, and she's wearing a blue cashmere sweater that suits her complexion and a pair of black leggings that wrap her curves. She's stunning.

"Hope you like soup." I give her a hot bowl when she sits on the stool on the kitchen counter.

"Thank you." She grabs it and digs the spoon into it. At the first bite, her eyes close, and a moan escapes her lips. "Oh, my God! This is amazing. Did you put wild garlic in it?"

I smile at her in surprise. It's a pretty unusual ingredient, considering she's from a ginormous city where you can get the most exotic fruit but hardly anything that grows in the mountains around those skyscrapers.

"How do you know that flavor?" I'm genuinely curious.

She shrugs her shoulders while she swallows another bite of soup. "I graduated from the Culinary Academy in New York, and I learned a lot about edible herbs to use in the kitchen." She appears almost melancholy talking about it.

"You're a chef?"

Olivia shakes her head. "I'm a—she frowns and corrects herself—I *was* an editor at Taste and Dream publishing."

"You *were*?" I can't stop myself from asking. I don't know why, but I'm surprised to discover that she is, or was, in the New York culinary scene. It's an insanely competitive industry, and she must have some balls to even think about that career.

"It's a long story, and it sort of explains why I'm stuck here with you." She smiles, but it never reaches her eyes, and she doesn't add any further explanation.

I don't ask for more. I'm not one to stick my nose in somebody else's business. We have weeks to talk about it, and the thought makes my heart sink in my stomach. What the hell am I doing with a complete stranger in my house?

# Chapter 5

Deciding to sleep in the living room in front of the fireplace last night was the best decision ever. Noah suggested I take his room, and he could spend the night on the couch, but considering the furniture's size and *his* size, it was clear he wouldn't fit.

The warmth of the fireplace and the crackling of the fire lulled me into a deep, restful sleep.

I smile, enjoying the warm thick blanket over my chest, and when I open my eyes, it takes me a few seconds to understand what is going on. Two small red eyes are staring back at me, a yellow beak in between them, and a red crown topping the tiny head. I'm so startled it takes me a long moment to grasp the fact that a bird is resting on my breasts, staring at me like a stalker.

A shrill sound escapes my throat as I hop up onto the armrest of the sofa. The poor little guy gets so scared he starts to flap his wings and scrambles for the

opposite side. Adding to the chaos, Jack starts barking at the sudden commotion in the living room, and Noah rushes down the stairs in just his boxers.

Well, that was quite a wake-up.

"What the hell happened?" he asks in a gruff-sleepy voice.

I move my gaze from the rooster to the guy in front of me. My mouth dries instantly. He is ripped. His pecs are two solid rocks dusted with short dark hair. His abs are so sculpted you could climb on them, with a dark happy trail in the center of the perfect V of his hips descending from his belly button down, down, down, disappearing under his tight-fitting boxers.

His legs are the size of tree trunks, but my eyes stare at the bulge of his morning wood that pairs perfectly with the size of his body.

I realize I'm staring, mouth open, at his private parts when he snatches the bird from the back of the couch with his huge hands and covers his crotch with it.

I return my gaze to his face where his eyes are fixed on mine, one eyebrow raised in a scolding arch. The sight of him hiding his cock behind, well, a cock, is so funny I can't stifle the laugh erupting from my chest.

"Sorry, I woke up with the little guy resting on my torso staring at me. I got startled," I explain.

He relaxes a bit, and a smile tugs at the corner of his mouth. "Sorry about that. Sometimes he sneaks in through the dog door and wanders into the living room. He's never attacked anyone, though."

It's my turn to raise an eyebrow. "Do you have a lot of people crashing on your couch at night? How do you know he doesn't attack?"

Noah opens his mouth and closes it, not knowing how to answer. "Well, if you don't mind, I'm going to put on something." He beckons his head toward his naked chest, and I can't stop drooling over the piece of art that is his body.

"Nice cock, by the way!" I can't help but tease him, seeing his discomfort at being naked in front of a stranger.

He groans without saying a word, and I smile. Usually, it takes a while for me to interact with people I meet, but nothing about this situation is normal.

He walks awkwardly toward the stairs, never letting go of his feathered friend. When he realizes he can't go upstairs with the bird, he puts him on the wooden banister and rushes upstairs, taking two steps at a time. I take this chance to go to the bathroom and put on something decent before he comes back.

When I come out, I find him dressed in a pair of loose gray sweatpants and a white t-shirt. The little guy is still in his hands.

"I'm going to put him back and grab some fresh eggs," he mumbles before stepping around me to reach a hidden door I hadn't seen near the bathroom.

"Do you have a chicken coop?" My eyes widen. I thought I was going to eat dried meat and soup for the entire winter.

Wendy Ashford—The grump and the chef

He turns around and frowns, studying me. "Do you think I keep a cock just for fun?"

I shrug my shoulders. "I don't know. You live in a cabin in the middle of nowhere, isolated from the world for most of the year. I'm not aware of what's normal for *you*!"

He considers my words, then shakes his head like he's refraining from saying something. He isn't a man of many words. No surprise he's living alone without human contact.

"Well, I need something other than canned food to survive, so…" he explains, opening the door to a surprisingly warm garage.

There's a chicken coop against the far wall, and he probably needs to keep them warm during the cold weather. I study him while he sets down the rooster, grabs a basket, and picks up five eggs and puts them in it.

He opens a bag of chicken food and replenishes the basin, grabs the water bowl and empties it on a sink in the corner, and refills it with fresh water.

I observe, mesmerized by the care this massive guy is using not to harm those little chickens. He strikes me as someone who could take down a bear with his bare hands, and at the same time, grab those eggs with his huge fingers without squeezing them.

"What did you name him?" I ask when he turns around with the basket of eggs.

He frowns yet again. Does he always frown? It's not like I ask complicated questions or stick my nose in his business. It's just conversation, for Pete's sake!

"Rooster," he answers after a while.

"You named the rooster Rooster?"

"Yes, why?"

"Go figure. You have the imagination of a four-year-old." I smile, and I can see his lips tugging at the corner. He's smiling too, but he doesn't want me to see it. "What did you name the chickens? Chicken?"

"Actually, chicken-one, chicken-two, chicken-three, chicken-four, and chicken-five." He places the basket on the kitchen counter when we return to the cabin, grabbing a pan from the cabinet.

"Wow, you can count to five! You are a big boy!" I joke, and this time he can't hide his smile. A very beautiful smile that crinkles the sides of his eyes a bit, making him even more gorgeous. Damn. He really is handsome.

"Ha, ha, ha. Very funny. Do you want eggs for breakfast? Not that I have much more to offer." He glances at me questioningly.

"You know what? Go, take a shower. I'll make breakfast."

He studies me for a long moment. "You don't have to. I can take care of myself."

I roll my eyes. Is he always so guarded? "I'm offering. I like to cook, remember?"

Wendy Ashford—The grump and the chef

"Okay," he mumbles. "Everything you need is in the kitchen or in the pantry behind that door." He points at a door in the corner next to the fridge.

"Okay, boss!" I chirp, putting my hands on his muscled back and pushing him toward the restroom.

He mumbles something I can't understand, but he goes into the bathroom and I hear the shower running.

Half an hour later, he comes out with his hair still wet and his beard groomed and shiny with some sort of oil. He gives off the impression of being a tough, rugged lumberjack, but he takes care of himself. Unlike some desperate hermit living up here, letting himself go, he seems to genuinely enjoy his solitary life. He sits down in front of me on the stool at the kitchen counter and studies me while I put the food on two plates.

"Scrambled eggs topped with caramelized onions, bacon coated with apple and a maple syrup reduction, and hash browns from fresh potatoes—with a twist." I put his plate in front of him.

"With a twist?" He raises an eyebrow, questioning.

"I found a single sausage in the fridge; I minced it and mixed it in with the potatoes." I wink at him.

Both eyebrows rise in surprise. "And you were able to cook all this in a half hour from scratch?" He's clearly impressed.

It's my turn to frown. "What, like it's hard?"

He shakes his head and smiles without replying before diving into his breakfast. As soon he takes the first bite, a moan escapes his throat, and his eyes snap to mine.

"This is ridiculously good," he congratulates me, and I can't keep a smirk from forming on my lips.

"I told you, I studied to be a chef." I beam because it's the first time someone is impressed by my skills. Greg never wanted to try my "experiment," as he called my cooking. He wanted more traditional meals, which I found boring.

"Well, that money was well spent." He nods and gorges on another generous bite.

I sit next to him and start to eat in silence. I'm halfway done when he finishes, and he gazes cautiously at me.

"Are you not enjoying your breakfast?" he asks unexpectedly.

"No, I love it. Why?" I study his pensive expression. He's trying to figure me out.

"Maybe because you're just pushing the food around without actually eat it?"

I blush, looking down at my plate. "No, it's not... I mean..." I have no idea how to explain it, but he keeps staring at me, expecting an explanation. I inhale deeply and continue. "I don't want to stuff myself."

He's silent for a bit, then turns slightly toward me. "Why? It's crazy good. Why shouldn't you enjoy it?"

Wendy Ashford—The grump and the chef

"Because if I dive into it with gusto, people start making comments on my weight and suggesting I should eat less end exercise more," I confess, my cheeks going up in flames.

He scoffs. "Who the hell says something like that?"

*Greg.* "People I eat with."

He gazes at me, dumbfounded, his mouth and eyes wide open. "Why on earth would they say something like that?"

"Look at me! I'm fat. It's not like I have the body of a supermodel," I blurt out.

He studies me for a long moment, and I see something like anger flicker in his eyes. "You're a woman with breasts and an ass. Soft and curvy. What's wrong with that?"

I shrug, not wanting to venture into the topic of unrealistic beauty standards for women. "It's not a big deal. I just eat slow, that's all." I try to downplay the awkwardness of the moment.

"Well, it's a big deal to me. You should enjoy your meal," he says, standing up and going to the sink to wash his dish.

I move my gaze to my plate, and guilt stabs at my stomach. I'm his guest, and I give the impression I don't appreciate his food. It doesn't matter that I cooked it. He's sharing his supply for the winter with me. I should be more grateful. I take a sizable bite of my breakfast and close my eyelids, enjoying the caramelized onion flavor tickling my tastebuds. When I open my eyes, I find him studying me with an unreadable expression.

He helps me clean the kitchen after I finish eating. We're both silent. I'm not sure what to say after his outburst about my eating habits, so I watch him sit on his armchair after he puts a log on the fireplace, and I sigh out loud.

I wander around his cabin, bored to death after fifteen minutes. How can he spend months alone here doing nothing?

"What's in here?" I ask before opening a small door under the stairs. I don't want to stick my nose in his things.

"A bunch of stuff," he answers without looking at what I'm pointing at.

"Can I take a look at it?" I ask with my hand on the doorknob.

He shrugs one shoulder. "Sure."

I open the door, and I'm a bit disappointed. I don't know what I expected to find, but not a mess of the usual…stuff. It's *that* closet. The one every house has. It's like *that* drawer but bigger. It's where you put what you don't need anymore but are too scared to throw away. Then, when you have to move, you put it all in a garbage bag because you realize it's been there forever and you've forgotten all about it.

A dusty tennis racket catches my attention. Noah doesn't seem like the tennis-playing type. I grab it

from the stuffed shelf and realize it's small. Maybe for his girlfriend…or wife.

I turn around and study him reading his book. I can't understand why a guy like him is trapped here without a trace of a woman. Does he have someone in town? And how do they deal with months when they can't see each other? I can't ask those questions without being rude, but I'm dying to find out more about this mysterious man.

After an hour of digging around old objects, including a purple lava lamp and a set of golf balls, I find a box with nothing inside except a deck of cards. I can feel the smile spreading across my face and a surge of adrenaline rising in my chest.

"I found something we can do!" I shout from across the room at him.

Noah takes his eyes off his book. "I'm already doing something." He shows me the book.

I get up and walk over to him, showing him what I found. "I have something way more interesting we can do together." I sit down on the plush carpet and put the cards on the coffee table between us.

Noah gazes at me like I'm an annoying bug, then he sighs out loud. "Do you constantly need someone else to keep you entertained?"

"I'm a social person," I explain. "I need human contact from time to time."

"How long between 'time to time' do you last?" he growls.

"I have no idea. I'm always surrounded by people," I explain, starting to shuffle the deck.

"Awesome," he mumbles, rubbing his hand over his face.

"Don't be such a grumpy ass," I scold him.

He stares at me with a murderous glare, but then he puts his book down, accepting the cards I'm handing him. "What are we playing?" he asks.

"Poker."

He raises an eyebrow, studying me.

"What? Aren't you familiar with the game?" I wonder. Given that he lives here alone, maybe he doesn't engage in basic fun things like playing cards.

"I know how to play, it's just... You know what? Never mind. Poker is fine."

"We should make it more interesting. We should go for strip poker," I suggest, more to see his scandalized face than to actually play that version of the game.

He raises his eyebrow again, challenging me. "Are you trying to get naked here?" he asks.

"Not particularly. But it adds some fun to the whole thing."

"Can we do something else? Not a fan of unclothed time in front of a stranger."

I roll my eyes. "Okay, the winner can ask the loser a question, and we have to answer truthfully," I propose.

He sighs. "Can we get undressed instead? I changed my mind."

"Nope." I grab my cards and pout when I see them. They suck.

"You are terrible at poker, you know that?" he asks, pointing at my face.

Perhaps I'm a bit too expressive. I shrug. "When I was at the academy, we didn't care much. The fun part was getting naked, not playing cards," I explain.

He smirks. "Fair enough."

He shows me his cards, and I do the same. "I win," he says.

"Question. I promise I'll tell you the truth." I smile at him.

"No doubt," he whispers under his breath. Then, louder, he asks: "Why are you here? Not the 'pinkish key ring' story you already told me. The real reason you felt the need to come all the way from New York to a place like this."

I take a deep breath and decide to tell him the truth. I wasn't planning to spill all my secrets, but I owe him this one.

"My boyfriend dumped me and then fired me. Or he fired me and then dumped me…I don't know, it was all part of the same conversation, so I suppose the order doesn't matter. I needed some time to think about what to do. I have to find a new job, a new apartment. I was overwhelmed, and I came to the only place I knew I could find some peace."

He studies me intently. I notice he doesn't blurt out what he thinks like I often do. He takes his time, choosing his words carefully. "I'm not familiar with the company policy, but I'm pretty sure you can sue him and the publisher. If he fired you, I assume he was your boss or someone higher than you in the ranks."

"Why? To be humiliated again in front of a judge? I don't want to have anything to do with him." My voice is firm, even if my stomach clenches in a painful grip. When I think about how Greg treated me, I want to scream. Not because I did something wrong but because I didn't see it coming.

Noah doesn't say anything; he just grabs the cards and starts to shuffle them, tossing me my hand.

I win the next round. "My turn. Are you single?" I want to ask more, but I can't guess how he'll react.

"Yes," is his brief answer.

I wait for a juicier explanation, but it doesn't come. "Come on! I told you about my ex. More details?" I plead.

He smiles but doesn't give in. "No, I asked you why you were here, and you told me everything. I didn't ask for all those details."

I stick my tongue at him and pout.

"How old are you? Twelve?" he deadpans.

We keep playing and I get the feeling he won't say anything more. He wins the next round.

"Come on. Another question," I chirp, and he stares at me.

"Can we skip the question part?"

"No! That's the fun of this game!"

"Wasn't it getting naked?" He uses my earlier words against me.

"Do *you* want to get naked?" I challenge him.

He sighs, exasperated, and I smile. "Why did you work for a publishing company if you wanted to be a chef?"

I tilt my head and study him. In the past, playing with other guys, they always wanted me to get naked, or asked me the color of my underwear. Noah seems to take this game very seriously, asking questions that dig deep, really getting to know me.

"I needed money when I first graduated from the academy. I found a job that required cooking skills in order to edit cookbooks. I accepted it because finding a decently-paying position in a kitchen was difficult. I met my boyfriend there, who convinced me that opening my own restaurant in New York was impossible, so I just stayed where I was." The more I explain this to Noah, the more I realize that my occupation was just a safe way to avoid my fear of not being able to make enough money with my dream.

"So, you just stayed there? Because he told you to?"

He's angry, and I don't understand why. "No, I stayed there because he was right. I don't have the kind of money to invest in a new restaurant. There's no guarantee it would even work—and if it flopped, I'd be in debt for the rest of my life."

He nods, but he still seems angry. We play this game for a couple more hours, and I reveal a lot about my life. About my parents' divorce, Ava, and a couple more private questions. He continues to reply with one-word answers.

"Was your ex a guy or a girl?"

"Girl."

"Did she dump you, or did you dump her?"

"Her."

"Are you living here because of her?"

"Yes."

I try to be creative with my questions, but at least now I can assume that someone broke his heart, and he escaped here to heal. I have no idea how long ago.

When it's finally time to go to bed, he seems exhausted. I stare at the fire while the snow outside keeps coming down like someone up there decided to pour it all this week. I have no idea when I can go back home, but at least I don't feel as hopeless as I did yesterday.

I overhear a rustling sound coming from the far end of the couch. I look over and find Rooster staring at me. "You are a little creep. You know that, right?" I smile at him.

He tilts his head and settles down on the sofa. I guess I'm quite the news up here, if even the rooster seems interested in me.

# Chapter 6

I peel my eyes open and stare at the ceiling. Yesterday, I woke up startled by a shrill cry from the living room—not a great way to start my morning—but this silence is even more alarming. I peer at the clock on my nightstand. Eight. I slept longer than usual because Jack didn't come scratching at my door at six asking for his breakfast.

I don't even want to know why he didn't come, but I suspect the reason is the blonde sleeping downstairs. She showed up and disrupted every routine we had.

I strain my ear to listen to the wind outside. Still raging. I doubt it'll let up soon. Not that I can kick her out and let her walk to Pinecreek with all this snow. She'd die after the first mile. Either she'd freeze to death with those ridiculous city clothes or she'd slip and fall, breaking her neck. It's a great trek in the snow, even for me, and I'm used to endless walks. The prob-



The grump and the chef—Wendy Ashford

lem is she won't be gone for a while. Just the opposite: I'm stuck with her and her constant chattering for way too long.

I sit up and rub my eyes, then move my gaze down and stare at my erection straining against my boxers. "Shit," I curse under my breath.

It takes me five minutes and a lot of gruesome images conjured by my brain to make my morning wood disappear. When I'm finally decent, I put on some sweatpants and a t-shirt and open my bedroom door, listening for any noise. The fire is crackling, which means Olivia put some logs in the fireplace. But where is she? The answer comes like a slap in the face when I walk to the top of the stairs, glimpse downstairs, and see her round, firm ass in the air.

She's bent at the waist doing who knows what, and the blood drains from my face, rushing down below my belt. All my resolve to get a grip on my body flies out of the window. I could get lost for days in that perfect ass. I can't believe someone told her she's fat. I suspect it was that prick ex. Never met the guy, but I'd gladly punch him in the face.

I shake my head, trying to think about everything but her in that pose. I gaze around the room, and can't stop a smile from forming on my lips. Rooster is perched on the armrest of the sofa, staring with his head tilted to the side at the same view I have. *I don't blame you. I know the feeling.*



Wendy Ashford—The grump and the chef

I move my eyes to Olivia, and see Jack rolling and sticking his ass up like he's imitating her. God, three days and she has him wrapped around her finger. *Get a grip, Jack, you are ridiculous.* I can't help but scold him with a stern look. And I'm ridiculous, too, standing up here staring at her ass.

I announce my presence by clearing my throat, and her reaction makes my cock jerk to life in my boxers. She stands up, blond hair tied in a loose knot on her head, pink cheeks, and full lips parted. I bet she's gorgeous like that when she comes on a cock. *Where the hell did that come from?* God. I'm so screwed.

"Hello, Sunshine!" she chirps in that gleeful tone I've come to recognize.

I raise an eyebrow. Sunshine? Is she for real? "Princess," I mumble while I walk to the kitchen to pour my more-than-deserved coffee.

"Stop right there!" She grabs my arm before I can reach my wonderful, hot cup of happiness.

I turn around and stare at her. I'm pretty sure I appear like a serial killer right now, but the murderous glare on my face doesn't deter her. She's smiling like a maniac.

"What?" I don't even want to know what she has in mind.

"First, a good amount of water to rehydrate, then come in front of the fireplace with me and do some yoga." She walks to the kitchen and pours a tumbler of cold, not-so-tempting, tasteless water and puts it in my hand.

I stare at the glass, then at her, then again at the glass, and back at her. Does she think I'm going to do something like that? "Absolutely not!" I protest.

She crosses her arms under her tits, pushing them up. Oh, those beautiful, gorgeous breasts. It's hard to pull my eyes back to her face. When I do, I see the determination there.

"Are you going to have breakfast and then sit down for hours again, reading a book?" she asks in a scolding voice.

"It's precisely what I'm planning to do. I don't know if you noticed, Princess, but it's still snowing outside. There's not much I can do until the sky clears a bit."

"You know this is bad for your body, right? You should stay active even if you are stuck here. Your body is your temple, you should take care of it. Or you'll go out there to do, I don't know what, and end up pulling a muscle. I'm here now, and I can help, but what about when I'm gone? What if you hurt yourself and you can't get back inside and freeze to death? Nobody will come here to search for you until spring." She frowns while she scolds me. She is cute when she's all worked up.

"Jeez! You're sure optimistic about my survival skills," I counter.

"You're getting older, you know. You need to start taking care of your body before it's too late." She's all flushed now.

"You're not giving up until I do what you want, are you?" I ask, knowing the answer.

"Nope." She tries to hide a smug smile.

"Are you going to shut up for the rest of the day if I do it?" I hope she does.

"Yes!" I can see the lie on her face.

I tilt my head and pin her with a stern gaze. I can read her bullshit.

"I promise I will shut up," she insists.

"Are you crossing your fingers?" I'm sure she is.

"Nope."

God, she is really a bad liar. Worse than her poker playing.

"Okay. But I'm not doing it for hours."

"Baby steps!" She grins at me, her eyes wide. I already regret my decision.

I drink the water, shivering with disgust. I need coffee. A ginormous, hot cup of joe will help me not end up in prison for killing her. But she grabs my hand and drags me to the fireplace. She's moved the low table and my armchair and is using the plush carpet as a yoga mat.

"Take it slow," she orders before bending down at the waist and sticking up her ass.

Jesus, I can't do this with my erection awakening in my pants. I bend down, trying to imitate her pose, and every single muscle in my frame hurts in protest. "Are you sure you're not trying to kill me?" My voice comes out strained.

She turns her head toward me, her cheeks red. "The first time is always the worst, then you'll get used to it. Trust me."

"First time? Do you think there will be a second time? You're crazy!" I protest, but she laughs in response.

After an hour, when we finish this immense torture, my body aches in places I didn't know could hurt, and my erection is standing out like the Eiffel Tower in my sweatpants. I clutch a throw pillow from my armchair and put it in front of my raging cock.

"I need to go out," I blurt out when I realize there is no way to hide my body's reaction.

She frowns. "You can't go out right after exercise. You will go into shock."

"Trust me, I need to go out."

I turn around, leave the pillow on the floor, grab my boots, and put them on without a pair of socks. I seize my jacket and the beanie, and rush out of the door before I even have the time to zip it up.

It's fucking freezing out here. The snow and wind slash my face as I struggle to reach the side of the cabin where I'm more protected from this weather. When I

Wendy Ashford—The grump and the chef

reach the woodshed I built a few years ago to keep the firewood dry, I walk inside and swipe my gaze around.

"What the hell am I doing out here?" I whisper to myself, rubbing a hand over my face to get rid of the snow.

I'm pissed. This is my cabin, my house, my dog, my rooster, I shouldn't be hiding out here because of some woman who completely messed up my life. I should have stayed home instead of giving in to my conscience and checking the hunting hut three days ago.

As soon as the thought crosses my mind, I feel a pang of guilt hitting my gut. If I hadn't checked, she'd be dead by now, or at least starving and scared out of her mind. I don't want her to get hurt, but I don't want to hide out here either. I need to find a way to share my cabin with her without going crazy.

I take a deep breath, then two or three. I stare at my pants, and the tent is still there. Even my body is betraying me.

How is it even possible I'm still hard out here in the freezing cold? The image of Olivia bent over in front of me, and on all fours with her round ass way too close to my body, comes to my mind, and I groan.

"Not helping, dude. Not helping at all," I mumble while I try to heat my hands, tucking my fingers under my armpits.

Forty-five minutes later, I'm still freezing my ass off in the woodshed when I hear the door open, and see the blond mane whipped by the wind searching for me. Fortunately, my erection is sleeping right now.

"I was looking for you. Breakfast is ready if you want it." Her tone is hesitant. She's bundled up in that ridiculous unicorn jumpsuit, pink Uggs, and jacket.

"I'm coming. I need to…grab some dried logs for the fire." *Dude, forty-five minutes for some wood? Very smooth.*

"Do you need help?" she asks, puzzled, clearly not convinced by my explanation.

"No, go ahead. I'm coming." I try not to sound too annoyed.

She stays a bit longer, studying me like she's trying to figure me out, but then she turns around and goes back inside. When I hear the door close again, I grab some firewood and walk inside.

She's piled two plates with a stack of pancakes, bacon, and canned peaches glazed with what looks like sugar. One advantage of having her here is I get a decent breakfast. I normally stick with a cup of coffee and a slice of bread.

"You didn't have to do all this. I'm fine with my coffee." I smile at her while I sit down at the kitchen counter.

She shrugs and sits beside me. "It's not like I have a lot to do. I have no idea how you deal with all this snow. It's been three days, and I'm going crazy."

Wendy Ashford—The grump and the chef

I dig into the stack of pancakes and moan when I taste them. "I read a lot, and I do some work outside when it's not snowing. It's not like I'm stuck inside for months," I explain.

She takes a big bite of her food, and I'm happy she's not pushing it around the plate.

"What do you do during spring and summer?"

"Some random jobs in town. One day I'm helping fix a roof, another day, they ask me to join some squad cutting trees. I don't have a stable job. I like it—I never get bored."

She nods and swallows a bite with some coffee. "Do you live here, or do you rent something in town?" I can read the curiosity all over her face.

"I live here. It's like half an hour away, but I have the chickens to feed, and during summer, I keep a small garden where I grow vegetables for the winter. I need to be here year-round."

"You can all your own food? Really?" She seems surprised.

I laugh. "Yes, you're not the only one who can cook." I'm surprised to find I'm curious. "So, if you have the money to open your own restaurant, what kind would it be?"

She thinks about it, and I take my time watching her brow furrow, giving way to the two creases in the middle. She always does that when she's focusing on something. The fact that after three days I know her body language means I'm spending way too much time with her.

"I like to mix tastes, but not in a crazy way like the food in fusion restaurants. I like to pair things you don't normally put together. Mix tradition with something new," she tries to explain.

"Like bacon with maple syrup and apple," I suggest.

"Right. That was mostly a traditional breakfast, but with a twist. I like to experiment in that way. And I don't want one of those upscale restaurants with such tiny portions you have to order a pizza at home because you're starving. I want people who come to my place to *feel* at home. Eating good food, not super fancy food, chatting with each other, and having a good time." The faraway look in her eyes tells me she's daydreaming about this hypothetical place.

"Like a family restaurant with a twist." I smile when she lights up at my comment.

"Exactly!" She beams.

And just like that, she sucks me into this weird conversation I've never had with anyone. I don't like to talk to people because it's always hard to keep a conversation going. When you spend most of your life alone, it's difficult to have enough in common with anyone to have more than a superficial chat.

But Olivia seems curious about the basic things that go on in my life. Like how many times I feed the chickens or how I can the vegetables. She seems genuinely invested in learning something new.

Wendy Ashford—The grump and the chef

I peek at Jack, who's looking adoringly at Olivia while she animatedly explains how she once almost burned down her kitchen trying a new recipe, and I realize I'm not the only one here who's screwed.

# Chapter 7

One month. It's been one month since I ended up in this cabin, and the snow just keeps falling. Not like the first few days. We see the sun from time to time, but it's impossible to stray far from this place. One sunny day, I tried to reach the trail that goes down to town, but I couldn't even find it. I had a hard time not crying in front of Noah when the despair of it overwhelmed me.

It's going okay with Noah. He treats me well, but I can see his patience is running thin and I understand why. He's used to living up here alone, so to say I disrupted his routine is an understatement.

The only one who seems happy to have me here is Jack—perhaps because I let him sleep on the couch with me. And Rooster is happy, too, or at least he likes watching me every morning. We've reached an agreement: I let him stare at me while I'm sleeping, and he doesn't get to sit on my chest while doing it. He stays on the armrest of the couch, near my feet. I think the



Wendy Ashford—The grump and the chef

fact that Jack sleeps with me explains why Rooster doesn't come closer, but I like to think we understand each other.

My mother is freaking out. When Noah gave me his fancy, high-tech phone to call her—it doesn't browse the Internet, but at least I can ring my mother, since mine gets no reception up here—she was so upset she wanted to deploy the National Guard to come rescue me.

I had a hard time convincing her I was safe with the guy she called *a serial killer in the making*. I laughed at her definition of Noah. He may be grumpy most of the time, but he's definitely not a serial killer.

Ava is freaking out, too, but for completely different reasons. When it slipped my lips I was stuck here with a hot lumberjack-looking guy, she begged me never to come back, to the make the most of this forced time together and have all kinds of fun.

She was ecstatic when I described him, and told me to take notes because when I get back—if I still want to go back—I have to describe in detail all the adult ways we entertained ourselves in his bedroom.

I smile, thinking about the conversation with my best friend, but it fades as I think about today. It's four in the morning on Thanksgiving Day, and I'm stuck here with a guy who doesn't acknowledge an ounce of festivity. Every day is the same with him. I don't even know what day of the week is if I don't check on my phone.

Yesterday, we talked a lot. I asked what he usually does on Thanksgiving, but he cut the conversation short, saying he's always alone and doesn't need to do anything out of the ordinary. He was particularly grumpy after that chat, and I think there's more, but I didn't want to pry.

Jack pushes his nose under my hand and huffs, dragging me out of my thoughts.

"You're awake, too," I whisper. "Should we do something for Thanksgiving?"

He stares at me but doesn't reply for obvious reasons. In the last few weeks, I've gotten used to talking to him, as Noah seems less and less inclined to have a conversation.

"We should do something to celebrate, right?" I try to convince myself this is a good idea.

I don't know if Noah is okay with that; this is his house, after all. But I refuse to sit here all day moping because I can't celebrate. I'm a social person. I love holidays where families fight and threaten to fall apart, but at the end of the day still love each other. Maybe Noah and I are just acquaintances, but we deserve to be happy today.

I sit up with a new resolve and walk straight to the pantry and the freezer he keeps there. I search for a turkey or some other kind of meat I can cook. No luck on the bird, but there's a nice piece of pork I can use.

"We're not going traditional today." I smile at Jack as he peeks at me, wagging his tail, waiting for his breakfast.

I grab all the food I can carry before going back to the stove and starting to prepare this banquet. But first, I replenish Jack and the chickens' food bowl.

****

It's ten in the morning when Noah comes downstairs and swipes his gaze around, wide-eyed, as though a bomb has exploded in his kitchen. When his eyes land on the table we never use that I've set for two, he frowns.

"What the hell…" he blurts out under his breath.

I walk around the counter, beaming like a kid who's just shown their parents some straight-A homework. "We don't have a turkey, but we can celebrate Thanksgiving!" I can't hide the excitement in my voice.

He raises his gaze to me, and the smile dies on my face. He is furious. "Why the hell did you do all this?" he spits angrily.

"I thought…" The words get stuck in my throat.

"You thought? I told you I don't celebrate Thanksgiving, but you did it anyway!" he shouts. "This is *my* house. You have no right to do whatever you want."

My heart squeezes in a painful vise. I didn't mean to overstep. I thought he just didn't do anything fancy because he's alone and it wasn't worth all the fuss. But this is different. There's something deeper underneath this overreaction.

"You wasted weeks of supplies for nothing."

My eyes snap to his. Is this why he didn't want to have a big meal? Because we don't have enough food? It makes sense. He stocked up for one person, not two. Tears start to fall down my cheeks and hiccups shake my chest. "Are we going to starve to death? We don't have enough food for two people, do we? Oh my God, I've killed both of us coming here!" Dread fills my chest. What have I done?

He appears taken aback, ashamed. He comes closer and reaches out his hand, but draws it back like he has no idea what to do. Like he's approaching a feral animal ready to attack. No doubt because I'm ugly-crying in the middle of his living room and I look like a mess.

"No, we are not going to die, okay?" he explains more calmly now. Regret fills his eyes.

"You just told me I wasted weeks of food!" I try to explain between hiccups.

He steps forward and grabs my arms, dragging me into an embrace. His reaction is so unexpected, so far from the Noah I've come to know during the last month, that I'm startled. It takes me a few heartbeats to hug him. He squeezes me to his chest, caressing my head with his massive hands. I feel his hard muscles under the flannel shirt, and I inhale his scent deeply. Smoke from the fireplace and soap. It's a masculine smell that belongs only to him.

"I'm sorry I overreacted." His chest vibrates with his deep voice.

82

"Am I eating all your food? Are we going to starve by spring?" My voice comes out soft, almost a whisper.

It's strange how his reaction made me cry, but now his strong arms make me feel so safe. It's like being hugged by a giant grumpy bear that wants to protect you. There's no more anger from before. Is he mad at me or not? Noah's confusing.

"We have plenty to survive, we won't starve."

"But you brought enough supplies for just one person, not two," I point out.

He puts his hands on my shoulders and pushes me back to gaze at me in the eyes. I already miss his comforting hug, and the heat of his body. "We have sufficient food to make it to spring. I always buy more than I need because you never know what will happen. Like a New Yorker crashing on your couch for months." His mouth curls up in a smile, and I'm somewhat relieved.

"I promise you that nothing is wasted. We can eat leftovers for a week, at least," I explain, and the shame returns to his face.

He guides me to the couch and sits next to me. "I owe you an explanation." He looks out the window and inhales deeply. "She left me at Thanksgiving."

He doesn't face me, but I don't need to see his eyes to know he's talking about the woman who broke his heart. The reason why he lives up here. The silence is so long I don't know if he'll say more, but then he turns to me, and I'm struck by the sadness in his eyes.

"We were going to be married on Thanksgiving. I waited for her at the altar for an hour, with all the guests squirming because she was way too late. When I realized she wasn't coming, I went home and found half of our closet almost empty, most of her stuff gone, and a letter on my pillow. She left because she was too young to start a family in the middle of nowhere. She wanted to explore the world, live in a big city, have fun, and live her youth to the fullest," he explains in a soft voice.

My heart breaks for him. I can't even imagine what it means to wait for the love of your life at the altar and never see her walk down the aisle. Jesus, I was humiliated because Greg dumped me and fired me at the same time. And let's be honest, after a month when the only thing I have to do is think, I understand now that I didn't love him. I was just *okay* with him. I felt safe in our routine, but I didn't have feelings for him.

"I'm so sorry," is the only thing I can whisper.

"It's okay. It's not your fault." He smiles at me, but it never reaches his eyes. "I can't blame her. We were both twenty-two, she was my high school sweetheart, and we'd never been with other people. I sort of jumped into the adult life, but she didn't follow me."

"Wait, you're thirty-two, right? You've been living alone up here for ten years?" I can't hide the disbelief in my voice and probably my face, seeing his sheepish smile.

84

"Yeah. Kind of a loser, huh?"

"No! A hell of a heartache!" I correct him. "And I never imagined all this celebrating could hurt you so much." I can't push the shame out of my chest.

He grabs my hand and squeezes. "It's not your fault. You didn't know, and I'm not the most chatty person."

A small laugh escapes my lips. "You can say that. I should call you Grump."

He laughs heartily. "I'm not that bad!"

I arch my eyebrow. "Are you sure about that?"

He smiles. "Okay. It is possible I'm not used to having people around, let alone living with me."

"Who force you to do yoga," I add, smiling.

"Yeah, that doesn't help either," he admits.

"What do you want to do? Throw away everything?" I ask, not sure what to do with everything I've prepared.

He frowns at me like I said I killed someone, and I blush in response. "No! Are you crazy? *That* would be a waste of food."

"Okay, so we eat but we don't celebrate? I can put on a disgusted face if you want." I try to cheer him up.

He erupts in another laugh. "We can celebrate if you want. What did you make? I woke up with my stomach growling at the smell in here."

"Pork roast stuffed with dried plum and nuts, mashed potatoes with homemade gravy, green bean casserole, and pumpkin pie. I also made a variation of a pecan pie because I didn't have all the ingredients for the original recipe. And…um…I don't know, a couple other things I can't remember. I started at four this morning, and my brain is a bit slow to catch up, right now." I realize he's watching me, wide-eyed.

"You know you're crazy, right? Why did you wake up at four to do all that?" he asks incredulously.

I shrug one shoulder and divert my gaze to my hands in my lap. "I couldn't sleep. Thanksgiving is always a big deal for me. I usually have three different celebrations to go to and this year is a bit…you know… strange." I feel guilty for wanting to celebrate while he feels like he's dying inside. It feels selfish.

Noah grabs my chin between his fingers and forces me to look him in the eyes. "It's okay to feel sad that you can't go home, you know that, right? I know this isn't the best day you've ever had, but I promise I'll try not to be a grump." He smiles.

"Don't promise something you can't deliver," I tease, and he smirks, standing and pulling me up by the hand.

He guides me into the kitchen and helps me finish the preparations. After a long silence, he asks, "So, tell me. What was your favorite Thanksgiving?"

I smile because I remember it like it was yesterday. "It may sound strange, but the one when I was ten, and my parents had decided the day before to get a divorce."

Noah turns to me, curiosity plastered on his face. "Really?"

I nod. "Every single holiday up to that one was a continuous fight between them. I was almost dreading November and December because I knew there'd be someone shouting and someone else shouting back. But that day, everyone was relaxed, and we had the most amazing day I can remember. My mom and dad had a good talk the previous day and realized they needed to split up. When that realization settled in, there was no more reason to fight."

He smiles and shakes his head. "I'm sorry."

"Don't be. From that day on, things were better. I somehow knew, even at ten, that it wasn't love between them. They got married young because my mother got pregnant and that's never the best reason to get married."

"And that's why you have three celebrations?" He frowns. "Why three?"

"Lunch with my mother, dinner with my father, and when I grew up, late-night cocktails with Ava, my best friend," I explain, and he laughs.

"Sounds like a busy social life!" He smirks at me, and I bump my hip with his. Or rather, my hip pushes his thigh, given the height difference.

"It is, but I like it."

"I noticed that," he mumbles.

And just like that, we settle into a comfortable chat about our childhood and the heavy weight on my chest this morning over not being able to celebrate with the people I love lifts. He makes me smile again.

I wonder if Noah is still sad about this day. He's smiling, talking, and somehow managing to slip out of his routine to do something for me. But I'm happy I can give him a new Thanksgiving memory to think about in the future.

He'll always remember the year that crazy New Yorker showed up in his life and made this day different than the usual pity party he'd been enduring for ten years. Maybe he'll smile about it too.



Wendy Ashford—The grump and the chef

# Chapter 8

*Olivia's breasts swing in front of my eyes while she rides my cock with slow, long circles of her hips. She closes her eyes, tosses her head back, and moans softly when I grab both tits in my hands and squeeze lightly, running my thumbs over her puckered nipples. Her hands rest on my chest as she ramps up and starts riding my cock with faster, hungrier strokes, driving me crazy.*

*She chases her orgasm while her long, soft blond hair swings over her shoulders. She is perfect. Her soft curves fit perfectly under my hands. Her ass is a piece of art, and her tits are every man's wet dream.*

*She opens her eyes and looks at me. I get lost in those sweet doe irises. Her pouty mouth opens slightly when she moans my name, and her pussy squeezes around my cock. Her orgasm is long and savage, and mine is coming up fast, strong, uncontrollable.*



The grump and the chef—Wendy Ashford

I wake up with a start and sit up, breathing hard after the most vivid erotic dream I've ever had. Holy shit! Sweat runs down my temple and my naked chest. My legs are tangled between the sheets, and I can hardly catch my breath.

"What the hell!" I whisper, rubbing a hand over my face.

It's no mystery that I find Olivia attractive. She's physically everything I like in a woman. Round ass, full tits, pouty lips, and huge, sweet eyes. But she's annoying as hell with her constant chattering, smiling, and relentless positivity. And she's from New York, a place I hate just for existing, and where she'll run back to after this precarious situation ends. But damn, she is gorgeous, and my erection seems to agree with me.

I look down at my boxers; there's no chance my cock is going soft after a dream like that. There's a wet spot from my precum—fuck! I almost came in my dream. Is that even possible?

I get up and throw on a pair of sweatpants and a t-shirt. It's six in the morning; she's probably still sleeping. Especially since yesterday, we celebrated Thanksgiving and stayed up late. I don't know how I feel about that. I've hated that holiday since my ex dumped me at the altar, but I have to admit yesterday was fun, and I didn't think about her even once. It was a nice change from the mood I've had in past years. On some level, I'm happy Olivia didn't listen to me and

dragged me out of the downward spiral I was falling into.

I walk downstairs, making as little noise as possible. Olivia is still sleeping on the couch, Jack curled up at her feet and Rooster is sleeping on the back of the sofa. Those three have the strangest friendship I've ever seen. In one glance, she connected with Jack, and he fell for her. He's usually a trusting dog, but not *that* trusting. It's like she has him under a spell. Not to mention Rooster. The little guy has never spent so much time in here.

I walk to the fireplace and revive the fire by putting a log on the embers. Jack perks up an ear and opens one eye, but then promptly goes back to sleep. Olivia doesn't even stir. She's asleep on her back, the blanket down at her hips and her arms over her head, making her t-shirt crawl up, showing her bare stomach. My dick jolts at the sight, and that's my clue to go to take a shower. A very cold one.

After ten minutes under the freezing water, my erection is still very much alive, so I decide to take care of it in a different way. One that makes me ashamed, but it's the only solution to this embarrassing reaction of my body. I'm thirty-two, for fuck's sake! I should be able to control my body.

I switch to hot water, lather my hand with soap and squeeze it around my cock thinking about Olivia's round ass while my orgasm mounts at lightning speed.

I'm enjoying it so much I take my time, prolonging the torture.

A loud bang on the door, followed by a squeal and a plea, startles me. "Noah! I need to pee. Like, I *really* need to pee right now," she groans, banging on the door.

"I'm coming!" In more ways than she thinks.

"I need you out now!" she shouts, and the only thing I can do is shut off the water, throw a towel around my waist, and unlock the door.

As soon as the click of the lock sounds in the bathroom, she pushes the door open, rushes in, pushes me aside, and drops her pants to sit on the toilet and pee. I'm so stunned I don't even have time to react.

"Are you peeing in front of me?" I ask dumbfounded, turning around to give her privacy.

She groans in relief. "Trust me, I couldn't wait!"

"Are you serious?" My voice drips with disbelief.

"Well, in my defense, you didn't leave," she points out.

She has a point. Why didn't I just walk out of the bathroom? I groan in response.

"Is that an erection?" she squeals.

My eyes snap to the bathroom mirror where she is staring at the massive tent under my towel. It's barely covering my cock.

"Were you masturbating in here?" she asks, her eyes widening when I don't answer.

Wendy Ashford—The grump and the chef

I'm so stunned by this situation I can't even move or speak.

"Oh, my God! You were masturbating in the shower!" she squeals, grinning.

That's it. I'm completely mortified. "I was not!" I totally was. I was thinking about her while fisting my cock. Damn, I need to leave this freaking bathroom. I grab the handle and open the door, walking out.

"You know that's totally normal, right? You shouldn't feel embarrassed. I do it all the time!" she shouts, laughing, while I close the door.

"For fuck's sake," I whisper under my breath while I walk to my bedroom. I didn't need to know that she takes care of herself while she showers. Now it's the only thing I'll think about every time she's in the bathroom.

I dry myself with the towel and get rid of the soap still clinging to my skin. I need to take another shower soon. Luckily, my erection softened and I can put on some clothes without looking like a perv. When I walk down the stairs again, she's already dressed.

She gives me a cup of coffee with a smirk plastered on her face.

"Drop it!" I point a finger at her face hoping to intimidate her.

Of course, she's unaffected by it. On the contrary, she keeps on grinning like a crazy woman.

"What? I didn't say anything." She's all innocence, batting her eyelashes.

"I can see you're dying to tease me," I grumble.

"Who? Me? I am not!" She pretends to be offended.

I raise my eyebrow, pinning her to the spot with a glare. "Go ahead. Say what you want to say. You will anyway."

She laughs, and my dick stirs in my pants. Great. "It's way too easy to get under your skin." She sips her coffee. "But I meant what I said earlier. It's normal. I didn't expect you to be completely asexual just because you live up here alone. You're a healthy young man. It would be strange if you didn't masturbate," she continues in a serious tone.

"Can we drop the subject?" I grumble.

"Why are you always so embarrassed? It's natural!" she insists.

"Because I value my privacy," I counter.

She scoffs. "We're forced to live together; I sleep on the couch for everyone to see, and we share one bathroom. There's no privacy in this house for two people who aren't in a close relationship."

She's right. This place was built with a single person in mind, or eventually, a couple who share the bedroom. Not two complete strangers.

"Or are you embarrassed because you don't have sex? Have you been celibate since she dumped you ten years ago?" Disbelief crosses her face.

Wendy Ashford—The grump and the chef

How the hell did we end up talking about my sex life? I shouldn't be surprised—Olivia always gets what she wants from me, one way or another—but this is utterly mortifying. "No! I'm not celibate!" I feel the need to defend myself, and it's irritating.

"Oh." She frowns.

Is she upset because I have sex? God, this woman is infuriating. "Oh?"

"I don't know why, but I'm surprised. I mean, you're hot, you probably have a lot of women throwing themselves at you, but you live up here like a caveman, and I thought…I don't know what I thought. I never imagined you having sex." She's still puzzled like she's trying to figure that out.

So, she thinks I'm hot. I have a hard time keeping my face straight. "It's not I'm like some kind of priest or waiting around for her. I have my needs, but when the weather's warmer, I'll go to a bar in a nearby town and pick up some woman to do just that. I don't do relationships. I'm clear that I want a one-night stand, and they agree they want the same. That's it." I don't know why I need to explain this to her.

"Why a nearby town and not the one you live in? It's easier to pick up someone you already know." She is genuinely curious.

"Because I don't want complications. I don't want someone I can see every time, who might expect something more from me."

She seems to think about this, and I start to squirm. This conversation is becoming more and more personal. I hate it.

"So, you don't do relationships? Why?"

I stiffen. "Did you miss the part where I was dumped at the altar?"

"It's been ten years. That's a long time to hold a grudge," she points out, raising an eyebrow.

Why am I even having this conversation with her? "Not many women are willing to live here, stuck with me for months on end without seeing another soul," I mumble.

She tilts her head like she always does when she thinks she has to teach me something. It's annoying how much I've picked up on her habits. "You could always live in town. It's so small it would be like living up here."

"If I live there, people expect me to have a social life, make conversation, go out of the house from time to time."

"And that's so difficult?"

"Yes!" I blurt out, turning around and walking to the garage where I keep the chicken cop.

Of course, she doesn't get the hint that I want to be alone, and she follows me. At least she drops the previous topic of conversation. "What are you doing?" she chirps behind me.

I glance at her and notice she's put on her ugly pink boots. She's here to stay. I take a deep breath. "I'm cleaning the chicken coop. You won't like it. Go in-side," I snap, hoping she'll do what I say. But of course, she doesn't.

"Why? Because I'm from New York?" She holds her chin up, daring me with her gaze to answer the question.

"No, because you always wrinkle your nose when I unclog the shower from your hair," I point out.

She makes a gagging noise. "That's disgusting."

I smirk because she's slowly walking backward. I laugh as I turn around and reach for the bucket to clean out the chicken cop.

"What is this?" she asks after a while. She was so quiet I thought she went back inside.

I turn around and frown. She's pointing at the cov-ered junk. "That's a snowmobile"

She makes a face I can't read, and then anger takes over her entire expression. I've never seen her like this. She's almost scary—a five-foot-tall bundle of fury marching toward me.

"Are you fucking serious right now? You've had a snowmobile for over a month that could take me to town, and it never occurred to you to tell me? Is it your master plan to keep me here?" she shouts in my face.

I put down my shovel and bucket. "Hold on right there. I don't have a master plan. That thing doesn't work. It broke down like seven years ago."

She frowns, her anger still brewing. Her arms are crossed below her breasts, pushing them up and driv-

ing my attention away from her face. It's difficult to return to her eyes, especially because they're so full of questions.

"What do you mean it doesn't work? You've never repaired it? Why?" Her tone is less angry now and more curious.

"No. I don't need it. I've never used it to go to town, so I didn't see the point of spending all my time on a thing I don't use," I explain, annoyance filling my chest.

Her face switches from anger to curiosity to concern. "What if you need it? What if you get hurt or sick and you need a doctor? That thing could save your life." It's like she's trying to convince me.

Anger boils in my veins. I don't need her preaching at me. I just want to live my life without worrying about someone else's concerns about how I live it.

"Nobody gives a shit if I live or not," I spit out. "If I get hurt, I'll die here, and nobody will care. There's no one waiting for me in town. There's no one calling me to check if I'm okay. It's just me, Jack, and these fucking chickens!"

I don't want to be angry with her, but she shoved the dagger deeper into a wound that never healed. When we decided to get married, we were so young that nobody else wanted to stick around to see us grow a family. All our friends went to college and had a life outside this place. When I lost her, I didn't have anyone else who cared for me. My parents were out of the picture a long time before that.

Her expression softens. "That's so… sad," she whispers.

"Well, sad or not, it's my reality," I mumble before walking past her and heading to my room.

I sit on the bed, my heart tightening in my chest. I didn't mean to leash out at her, but her being here is bringing life back into this cabin, reminding me of all the life out there I'm missing. The fact that I woke up this morning after dreaming about Olivia means she's crept under my skin more than I care to admit. And when the snow melts, she'll be gone, and I'll be alone again.

# Chapter 9

I open my eyes with the creepy sensation that some-one's been staring at me while I was sleeping. Considering Rooster's habit of watching me from the armrest of the couch, I shouldn't be surprised to find him in his usual spot.

"Good morning, little creeper," I murmur still half-asleep.

A snort and a chuckle from the fireplace causes me to sit up with a start and a yelp so loud Jack starts to bark.

"Why are you all watching me sleep? What's wrong with you guys?" My heart is jumping out of my chest.

"I wasn't watching you sleep. I was stoking the fire." Noah gestures toward the fireplace.

"Why? It's still dark outside! Don't you have any-thing else to do?" I'm still trying to figure out what's going on. Noah never wakes up this early.

100

"Like what? It's still dark outside," he counters with a smug smile.

I roll my eyes and frown as I watch him walk to the kitchen and start to make coffee, and take out some pans. What's he doing? Breakfast? I stand up and walk to the kitchen counter.

"I'm afraid to ask," I murmur when it's clear I'm right. He is cooking at the crack of dawn.

He glances at me, curves his lips in a smile, and then focuses on his task again. "I want to apologize for yesterday. I was rude to you, angry with someone else, and I shouted at you. It wasn't fair, and I want to make up for that."

"By waking me up hours before my normal time? Not a terrific start, dude," I point out.

He chuckles and shakes his head. "No, I want to take you somewhere, but we'll have to walk for a couple hours in the snow. I need you to be fed and ready. The weather forecast for today is exceptional," he says cryptically.

"So, you're trying to make me walk for hours in the snow with my barely appropriate winter clothes so I'll freeze to death, and you can bury my body somewhere? You know what an apology is, right?" I stare at him in disbelief.

He chuckles again, and it's the third time in twenty minutes. A record for him, considering I've only seen him smile about five times this month. Something's up here.

"God, you mean you don't just have blind faith in me?"

"You're acting like a psycho! I'm a little concerned."

He rolls his eyes and keeps frying the eggs. "I felt guilty for yelling at you, okay?" he admits.

I smirk. "So, you're not apologizing, you're just clearing your conscience!"

He stares at me, mouth open. "You are annoying, you know that? I'm trying to do something nice, and you're ruining it with your pessimism." He is totally messing with me.

I laugh. "I like to make you squirm."

"I noticed," he grumbles under his breath.

"But I appreciate the gesture. I yelled at you, too, but I was freaking out when I thought I could've gone home a month ago, and for some reason, you didn't tell me."

"Keeping you here for no reason would have been beyond creepy," he admits with a frown.

"Yeah, definitely. Like a serial killer move or something." I shiver at the thought. "Speaking of wanting to kill someone, can I borrow your phone to call home?" They know I'm alive, but I have to check in from time to time.

"Sure." He gestures toward the phone on top of a small cabinet in the living room.

Ava answers on the first ring.

"Do you have this number saved?" I ask. "You never answer this fast!"

"Of course, I do. If he's going to kill you, I have something to give to the police." I can hear the smile in her tone.

"Thanks for that. I think." I laugh. "I'm calling to let you know I'm still alive. Noah is feeding me, keeping me warm and entertained." I smirk when I see Noah rolling his eyes on the other side of the room.

"Yeah, yeah, this is great, but are you sleeping with him?" she asks matter-of-factly.

"Ava!" I feel my cheeks go up in flames. Jack perks up his ears from the spot on the couch where he's still napping.

"You said he's hot, and you're stuck together in a cabin with not a soul around. What are you doing all day? I mean, why not have some fun?" She doesn't sound like she is joking.

"Ava, I can't just jump…" I peek at Noah, who all of a sudden seems curious about this conversation. "…from one guy to another just like that!" I whisper-shout while shrinking into the couch, hoping Noah won't hear. I spy in his direction and don't miss the smirk on his face. Awesome.

"You don't have to marry the guy. You just have to ride him!" she points out.

It sounds easy, coming from her. She's gorgeous, skinny, and flawless. I'm a curvy girl whose ex asked me to cover up during sex because my wobbly body was unattractive. Not the best person to look to for self-confidence. And definitely not a femme fatale when it comes to seducing a man.

"Ava, stop. I'm not going there." Even if I do want to. He *is* really handsome. "Can you tell my mom and dad I'm okay? If I call them, they'll insist on sending the army to rescue me."

She scoffs. "You're asking me to calm down your mom? You know I'll need a week's worth of margaritas to recover from that trauma, right?"

I smile. She's right, which is why I always call my best friend and not my mother. She's a major drama queen. "I promise I'll make it up to you."

"Okay, but next time you call her. I need a break from her drama—for my own mental health," she grumbles.

"I promise. I need to go now," I say when I see Noah putting two plates on the kitchen counter.

"Olivia?" Ava sounds almost worried. "Promise me you won't throw away the chance to have fun with Noah just because you feel guilty about Greg? He's an asshole, and you deserve to be happy," she says sweetly.

I can't tell her this without Noah hearing it, but I haven't once thought about Greg since I laid eyes on the guy I'm sharing this cabin with. It's like my ex-boyfriend is someone I broke up with ages ago.

I think it's all this forced proximity that makes my head spin. When you have no choice but to live twenty-four-seven with a person, you start to develop feelings you can't explain. I'm attracted to Noah—God knows I'd jump him in a heartbeat—but it's not just that. I like his grumpiness, his laid-back ways, and his simple life. I like how he enjoys small things, like sitting on the couch scratching Jack's ears for hours while he's reading.

There are so many small things like that I'm forced to notice, and I like them. It's not just a physical pull I feel for him.

"I promise," I finally answer her.

When I reach Noah at the counter, he's already eating, and I notice he's still got that smirk on his face.

"What?" I sit down on the stool a few feet from him.

"She asked if we're having sex, didn't she?"

I almost choke on my coffee. "What?" I play dumb, but he totally nailed it.

"You're not so good at whisper-shouting into the phone," he chuckles. "It doesn't take a genius to understand what she asked you. Especially when you turn redder than a tomato."

I cover my face with my hands to hide my embarrassment. "I could kill her sometimes!"

Noah chuckles again but gives me a break and lets the topic go.

"Where are we going today? You know I'm not equipped to walk long distances in this snow," I ask. Curiosity is eating me alive.

"I have a box or two of my ex's clothes in the back. You're about the same size. I'm sure you can find something to wear," he says with a neutral expression.

After ten years he still keeps her clothes in a box? A pang of disappointment hits me like a punch in the gut. I don't know why I was expecting anything different. He's been living like a hermit up here for ten years, so clearly, he hasn't gotten over her. But what surprises me the most is that I'd hoped he'd forgotten about her, and that realization is terrifying.

I can't fall for a guy who lives in the middle of nowhere with no intention of moving on from a past relationship. As Ava said, I should have fun, but fun doesn't include the disappointment of his emotional unavailability.

"Okay, sounds like a plan!" I say way too enthusiastically to sound genuine.

He studies me, frowning, but says nothing.

***

The walk in the forest wasn't as bad as I expected. Noah gave me a pair of snowshoes to wear with his ex's boots that miraculously fit my average-sized feet, and the trek was definitely more comfortable than my walk from the hunting cabin to his.

The forest appears to be almost magical under the sun. The high trees are covered in several inches of white powdery snow. The light reflecting on the tiny crystals where the massive pine trees clear is almost

blinding, even with our sunglasses on. The freezing air fills my lungs, cooling me down after I'd begun sweating in the warm clothes Noah gave me.

We don't speak much. A rarity for me, but I'm appreciating the silence of the snow-covered forest. Noah sometimes points to a small animal that, most of the time, I miss, or at some other peculiarity of this place. I could spend hours listening to him explaining the things he loves: this place and the wildlife in it.

We reach our destination a couple of hours later, and I'm completely breathless at the view. Surrounded by mountains and forest sits a small, snow-covered lake that seems to be right out of a fairytale.

"Wow, this is…" I'm so stunned by the sight I can't even finish the sentence.

Noah chuckles. "So, there is something that leaves you speechless. Good to know." I can't see his eyes behind the dark lenses, but I know they're a vibrant green when a genuine smile appears on his face. It's a rare sight but sometimes I catch it, and it's precious.

I stick out my tongue as I watch him take off his backpack.

"We're going fishing today," he states.

"We're doing what? The lake is frozen!" I wave toward the expanse of snow.

Noah stops what he's doing and studies me. "You know that's just on the surface, right? It's not a huge chunk of ice all the way to the bottom. There's life below the frozen part."

He explains it the same way a teacher would do, like he really thinks I don't know this, but I can see he's struggling to keep a straight face.

I arch my eyebrows and cross my arms to convey my no-shit-sherlock vibe. "Are you sure we can walk on there? If we end up in the water, we'll die," I point out.

He finally smiles and picks up an auger from his backpack. "I think we're safe, but we'll check if the ice is thick enough. If it's thinner than four inches, we won't walk on it."

I watch as he puts one foot on the ice and tests it, then walks a couple of feet in and starts to cut a hole, measuring the ice. He beckons me to follow him, and keeps doing it every few feet.

I'm so focused on watching him work I don't notice we've reached the middle of the lake. When I move my eyes away from the frozen surface, I'm in awe. We're surrounded by snow, and a little far away, the tall pines, and behind that, the huge mountains. It's like we're in a massive basin, and we're just specks of dust. I feel small and protected by the trees and mountains at the same time.

"Now I understand why you live up here," I whisper, careful not to disturb the quiet of this place.

"It's what I like most about living here." He starts to clear the snow from the lake's surface.

I watch him taking off his snowshoes to walk on the ice. "Do you come here alone? Aren't you worried

something might happen, and you'll end up dead?" I've been having those thoughts a lot lately. He's truly, utterly alone here. If, for some reason, he gets hurt, he has no one to help him. He didn't get a single phone call this month. No one is checking in on him.

"What's wrong with you? Why are you always thinking I'm going to end up dead?" He smiles, but it's a tired one.

"I'm worried I'll see your face on the news some-day because they found your frozen, half-eaten body somewhere around here!" I blurt out, and he frowns.

"That's quite a gruesome image you've got of me. Why half-eaten?" He's teasing me now.

"Because of animals?" I wave my hands around at our surroundings. The wildlife would have a field day with his flesh. And that's lot of beautiful flesh, mus-cles, and body I want all in one piece!

He laughs while he helps me take off my snowshoes. "Trust me, I'm completely fine. I've survived up here for ten years. I'm not going to die anytime soon."

I put a foot on the ice and start to slip. Noah grabs my elbow, but I wave my arms to keep my balance, throwing him off balance and ending with us both sprawled on the hard icy surface—Noah on his back and me on top of him, facing down.

His hard body under mine is paradise. He hugs me tightly, my hands resting on his chest. He winces in pain, then looks me in the eyes and his expression turns almost feral. There's an undeniable lust there I've never seen. His sunglasses have slipped up on his forehead, and I can see all the emotions running through those green irises. We're so close I can feel his hot breath on my face.

I think he wants to devour me, and not in a bad way. And the scary thing is, I'd let him do it. He reaches out a hand and moves a lock of hair from my face. His touch is gentle, but it seems like he's struggling to keep his hands to himself.

"You know what?" He startles me with his raspy voice.

"Huh?"

"Forget what I said before. I'm not safe up here. *You are going to kill me!*" He laughs, but there's more than one meaning in his words. He's referring to this fall, but I'm sure the lust I saw in his eyes has something to do with him thinking he's not safe.

I stretch my neck down, reaching his cheek. His eyes widen, and he stops breathing. "You know, I can always be your personal, loving nurse if you need someone to take care of you," I whisper seductively in his ear before kissing his cheek. I've never been this bold with a man. Ava would be proud of me.

I sit up and look at him as he stares at me like he's never seen me before. It's like something snaps inside him, and when he sits up, he grabs my waist and drags me to him, making me squeal in surprise.



Wendy Ashford—The grump and the chef

"Careful what you're offering. I might just hurt myself on purpose to find out how good a nurse you are," he growls in my ear, and my body resonates with that warning. My nipples harden under my sweater, and my pussy clenches in response. I've never been excited by the deep rough voice of a man, but to be honest, I've never met anyone like Noah before. When he stands up and helps me to my feet, my body feels like a shaken can of soda, ready to explode. Something shifted and changed on this ice, and it has nothing to do with the fall.

***

We're sitting on the couch after dinner, and I'm sipping my hot chocolate. We stayed at the lake all day, fishing, chatting, and having fun. Genuine fun, the kind that makes your belly hurt from laughing and your cheeks sore from smiling. We didn't talk about the moment we had on the ice, but a there was definitely a subdued tension in the air. And something buzzing deep in my lower belly, making me shiver with anticipation from time to time.

"We fished and ate the best trout in the world, and now you're ruining that perfection by drinking hot chocolate?" Noah makes a disgusted face that's almost comical.

"I need dessert after dinner, okay? But I admit that trout was fantastic. I had no idea you could cook fish like that. You'll have to teach me how you make it."

He smiles coyly. "We'll see. We'll have to go fishing again if you want me to teach you."

"Well, why not? We are the perfect fishing team. We're unstoppable."

"Shut up!" He laughs. "You didn't think we'd catch anything, and you kept talking and moving around the whole time, scaring off the fish. We're the worst team ever."

I put my empty cup on the coffee table and turn my body completely to face him. "That is not true! You fish, and I keep you entertained while you'd otherwise be bored to death waiting for some fish to bite. I'm the best support fisherman who ever existed," I point out, placing my hand on his muscular, perfect shoulder and pushing him. Or at least I try to push him, but he's so massive I can't even move him an inch.

He tenses under my touch but doesn't budge. "Sure, if you say so," he smirks.

"Are you implying I'm not the perfect support fisherman?" I pretend to be horrified.

He snorts. "There's no such thing as a support fisherman."

"Are you saying I'm a liar?" I gape at him.

"You said that, not me."

I try to push him again, but Noah grabs my wrist and drags me to him. Like this morning, the air around us gets charged with a buzz I recognize as lust and desire. I think back to Ava's words, to not pass up this chance to have fun with him, and I relax against his chest.

Wendy Ashford—The grump and the chef

"Stop pushing me," he warns in a raspy voice.

My lower belly clenches. "Or what? Are you going to put me on your knee and spank me?" I raise my eyebrow, daring him to do it.

Lust flares in his green irises, and his free hand gropes my ass, hauling me to straddle him. He frees my wrist, and his fingers dive into my hair, grasping a fistful and dragging my whole body to his chest. I can feel him hardening under the thin layers of our clothes against my core. Our breathing is ragged, and when I stare into his eyes, lust and desire almost burn me alive. God, he is like molten lava running under my skin, in my veins, making my body hot and ready for him.

We stay like that for what feels like too long, and then his lips crush mine, my world surrenders to his assault, and my core spasms against him. I want him, I want every part of him. His mouth, his tongue, his strong hands, and his broad chest. I want him all over me.

His tongue slips into my mouth, and a moan escapes my lips when he deepens the kiss. It's rough, primal, so savage that every cell in my body resonates with lust and desire.

Holy shit! This guy can kiss. Better than anyone I've ever kissed! He possesses my mouth with slow, potent strokes that awaken all my senses, and when I dig my hands into his hair and grab a big chunk of it, a groan rises from his chest that makes my whole body vibrate.

I whimper at that sound. I'm so turned on I freaking whimper! Then I moan in protest when he leaves my mouth, but it lasts just a few seconds because when his lips start to feast on my neck, my world shifts again.

"Oh, my God!" I breathe, dry-humping his massive erection.

I'm going to come in my panties like a teenager. But Noah suddenly freezes. It's like his entire body tenses under my touch. He pulls away, and when I scan his eyes, I see guilt and regret. It's like a cold shower, and every part of my body cries almost in pain.

"Sorry, I shouldn't have. I…I need to go." He moves me over on the couch and stands up like his seat is on fire.

"What?" I blurt out when he's already on the stairs storming to his room. He doesn't even reply, let alone look me in the face.

I sit down, turn around, and face the fireplace. And now I see what put the wall of ice between us. Sitting in front of the fireplace to dry are his ex's boots I wore today, a glaring reminder of why he lives up here. Yeah, I knew it was too good to be true. If I had any doubts about whether he was getting over his ex, this is the answer I didn't want to see.

Wendy Ashford—The grump and the chef

# Chapter 10

It's four in the morning, and I'm already awake. I barely slept, thinking about what happened not even six hours ago with Olivia. I can't believe I kissed her. And I wouldn't have stopped if I hadn't seen those boots—a stark reminder that women never stay in my life. Olivia's no different. When this is all over, she'll go back to New York, and I'll be here licking my wounds for another ten years. Because she's not some random chick I picked up in a bar and never see again after we had sex. I'm living with her, for fuck's sake!

Like it or not, our relationship is far from my usual one-night stands. Kissing her, sleeping with her—because I can't hide it, last night I would've totally fucked her—changes everything. And I'll be the one getting hurt. Again.

I sit up and stare at the alarm clock on my nightstand. It's four-thirty, way too early to go outside, but the urge to do something to get away from her is almost



The grump and the chef—Wendy Ashford

unnerving. This is my home. I should enjoy being here, but this place has become almost suffocating lately. I put on some clothes and tiptoe out of my bedroom, trying to be as quiet as possible.

When I get downstairs, Jack perks up his ears but he doesn't stir. Olivia is sound asleep on the couch. She's so beautiful it almost hurts. She's curled up under the blanket, her hands under the pillow, her lips slightly parted. I swear, those lips will be the death of me.

I walk to the garage and, after feeding the chickens, turn my attention to the snowmobile, taking off the dusty cover and inhaling deeply. I should have fixed it years ago, but I never saw the point in it. I don't need to go back to town. But I should probably end this agony sooner rather than later. Before I get hurt. Before Olivia realizes this situation is insane and doesn't want anything to do with me, while she's still stuck here.

I have no idea what's broken, but taking it apart and putting it back together sounds like a great place to start. So, I grab my toolbox and start what I should have done years ago.

Three hours later, Jack comes in, his tail wagging. He sticks his nose under my arm, reclaiming my attention.

"Now you want to cuddle? It's been over a month since you left me for the blonde sleeping on the couch," I grumble when I'm forced to put down the screwdriver I'm holding.

Wendy Ashford—The grump and the chef

He wags his tail faster, and I can't resist scratching behind his ears. Pieces of the snowmobile are scattered on the floor and though I'm far from being done, I need to take a break.

If Jack's here, that means Olivia is awake and probably showering. I get up, walk into the house, and hear the water running in the bathroom. I make coffee and pour some into a thermos, then put on my boots and jacket, ready to go out again. When I open the front door, Jack follows me.

"You can't come with me. It's way too cold for you to stay out all day." I try to push him back inside. He whines, but when he feels the cold air, he steps back. I close the door and inhale deeply.

Why the hell am I running from my own house? The answer is something I don't want to face.

***

The fallen tree trunk in front of me is almost completely bare. I cut off all the branches I can handle without a chainsaw, going at it for hours until my muscles scream in pain.

I'm sore, drained, and starving and my mind hasn't drifted for one second from that kiss. Because, damn, that was an amazing kiss. I loved every single minute of it. Her soft lips, her tongue darting in my mouth, her sweet chocolate taste, and those moans escaping her throat. I was almost gone at that point, but when she started humping me, I lost my mind.

She's so perfect, so damn cute and cheerful and clever. The first time I saw her, I thought she was some airhead city girl needing an adventure. Now I know she's not like that at all. She has dreams, and she's smart. She loves the Pacific Northwest because it gives her a break from city life, something I never thought could be attractive in a woman. She's a girl who, under normal circumstances, I could have fallen for. But nothing about this is normal, and I can't go down that road.

I check my watch and sigh when I realize I've been out here almost eight hours. I haven't eaten since dinner last night, and I worked my ass off for nothing because I don't even need the firewood. I've been stocked up since summer.

The sun is already going down, and I'm half an hour from the cabin. This was a stupid thing to do. I could faint or get hurt and die out here. You can't make stupid decisions when you live alone surrounded by snow, not even to avoid a sexy blonde living in your house. What would she do if something happened to me? I feel a bit guilty as I grab my things and trek back to the cabin.

When I open the front door, I'm greeted by Jack wagging his tail and whining loudly. "Hey, buddy, I'm home. Stop crying," I mutter, scratching behind his ears.



Wendy Ashford—The grump and the chef

"Where the hell have you been?" The angry voice makes my gaze snap up to Olivia, who is standing up from the couch.

I'm confused by her puffy red eyes and nose. Is she crying? Why? "I was out chopping some wood," I grumble, not wanting to go deep into the explanation.

"For almost nine hours? Why? You have a shed full of firewood!" she shouts.

"Well, I need more!" I shout back, knowing I'm just trying to spin my bullshit actions. I shouldn't have stayed out all day.

She storms toward me and pushes my chest with her small hands. I'm so stunned by the gesture that I stumble back and hit the front door I just closed. She is furious. Jack starts to whine and bark, alarmed.

"You didn't leave a message, nothing. I was terrified!" she shouts, tears streaming down her face. "I didn't know where to come to look for you. I wandered outside around the house calling you, but I was too afraid I'd get lost if I tried to walk farther into the forest. And I didn't even know which direction to go, because there's no way I can track you down when it's snowing. At some point, I almost called 911 to get someone to rescue you!"

I grab her wrist and pull her to my chest. I'm an idiot. I'm so used to living alone that I didn't think she'd be worried about me. I didn't think at all about what she was going through. I'm a huge asshole—making her cry like this, worried sick about me. I hug her tightly, her arms clenched around my waist, her face sobbing into my jacket.

"I'm sorry, I didn't think you'd be worried. I didn't think at all," I whisper.

"Why did you go for the whole day without telling me?" she asks between hiccups.

"I…" I don't even know where to start. "I was avoiding you."

That gets her attention. She peels off my chest and peeks at me, frowning. "Wait, you were what?" She's stunned.

I take a deep breath while I remove my boots and jacket and go to put some logs on the fire. It doesn't need to be stoked, but I need to do something. Anything but look her in the eye. Shame starts filling my chest.

"I was avoiding you," I repeat with a sigh.

"Because of what happened last night?" she asks, disbelief dripping from her words.

"Yeah, sort of." It was totally that.

She grabs my shoulder and turns me toward her, even more furious than before. "So, you make me worry all day, driving me crazy in here because you don't have the balls to talk about a stupid kiss?" She's shouting again.

"Well, it wasn't so stupid to me," I counter, a bit disappointed she doesn't feel the same way I do about it.

Wendy Ashford—The grump and the chef

"It's stupid compared to what you did afterward. I'm talking about the fact that you could've died out there!" She's almost trembling with fury. I didn't think a person could even be so angry.

"You're overreacting. You're such a drama queen!" I don't even know what I'm saying right now. This whole situation is a complete mess.

She scoffs, crossing her arms. "You disappear for nine hours into the forest because you can't handle a conversation about what happened, and *I* am the drama queen?"

Well, when she puts it like that…

"You want a confrontation? Here you go! Are you going back to New York this spring?" I ask, staring down at her.

She frowns. "Of course, I'm going back. I can't just stay here and live with you. I have a life there."

I feel like an idiot. And maybe a bit crazy because she's right. What am I asking her, exactly? To live with me? To give up everything and stay here in a cabin? That kiss made me think—a lot. About my living situation, my decisions.

There's a whole world out there I'm avoiding. But at some point, it will come knocking at my door, reminding me that I wasted my life hiding instead of trying to heal my wounds and step out there again.

Olivia and that kiss are both a stark reminder that I'm overthinking and rushing to conclusions that don't make sense—all because I've built this precarious fortress around me. And it took just one kiss to almost topple it.

"So, yeah. That kiss is a huge problem!" I turn and storm up the stairs to my room, putting some distance between me and her stunned face.

***

It's one in the morning when I finally give up and walk out of my bedroom. I'm starving. I spent hours thinking about our fight, and I feel so stupid about everything I said and did. I want to hide in my bedroom for the rest of the winter. But that's exactly what I did, right? I hid up here when things got hard ten years ago.

I try not to make a sound with Olivia sleeping on the couch, and when I open the fridge, I cringe as light floods the space. I take out some bread and cheese to make a sandwich.

"There are leftovers from my dinner if you want to reheat them." Olivia's sleepy voice from the couch startles me.

"Sorry, I didn't want to wake you up," I mumble, watching her walk to the fridge and take out a plate to put in the microwave.

The fireplace barely illuminates the room, but I can make out her sleepy eyes and the messy bun on her head.

"Can we talk about that kiss? It obviously upset you." She looks me in the eye.

Wendy Ashford—The grump and the chef

I take a deep breath and nod. "We should."

"I know you're not over your ex, but it really was just a kiss. I mean, I got dumped a month ago, I'm not jumping into a relationship just because I kissed you," she reasons, and everything she says makes sense.

"It's not about my ex. Or at least, not the way you think." I try to explain, but I don't know how not to sound crazy.

She tilts her head and leans against the counter. The shorts and t-shirt she sleeps in are way too distracting right now.

"You've kept her things in boxes for ten years," she points out.

I smile. "I don't know if you noticed, but we don't have a garbage truck that comes to take away the trash. I forget to take them to town during the spring. That's all."

"Okay, but you freaked out because of a kiss," she insists.

She's right. I completely lost it over a kiss. "I know I sounded crazy asking if you're going back to New York—I'm not some kind of lunatic that wants to lock you in the basement. But I was surprised by that kiss, and I started to overthink it. It's this living together that's messing with me. It's the first time I've lived with anyone since my ex, and I suddenly felt like we were jumping into something more than what we are— barely acquaintances. I felt overwhelmed and scared, because the last time I exposed myself like that, I got hurt. Badly." I blurt it all out, feeling vulnerable and foolish.

Olivia smiles and nods. "I can understand the overwhelmed thing. I think all this forced cohabitation is getting to our heads. Sometimes I wonder if I'm some kind of ho because I'm attracted to you instead of crying over my breakup. But then I think there's no rule for how long to wait to get over a relationship. It can be one month or ten years. It depends on the person and the situation. What I'm trying to say is, I'm taking things one day at a time, with no expectations. Maybe we keep kissing, and you discover that you don't like it, and then I'm the one who ends up with a broken heart."

I shake my head, but she's right. I have no idea what will happen, mostly because I was barely older than a kid when I gave up on relationships. "I highly doubt I will discover I don't like kissing you." I raise my eyebrow.

She smirks. Olivia is not someone to smile shyly and hide her embarrassment. She wears her emotions openly, and right now, she's smug. "So, you liked kissing me!"

"You could say that." My lips curve in a grin.

This situation may be completely messed up, but I can't deny I'm craving another kiss from her. Damn my overthinking, she's irresistible.

Wendy Ashford—The grump and the chef

"Good, because I liked it too!" She bites her lower lip, and my gaze is drawn there.

"Good, because I'm thinking of doing it again." I slowly close the distance between us and put my hands on the counter on either side of her, trapping her there. I lower myself until I can look her in the eyes. Lust heats up those huge fawn irises.

"Good, I want to be kissed," she whispers, lowering her gaze to my lips.

I crush my mouth on hers without hesitation. Damn all my thoughts and doubts. We both want this kiss, and I'm not going to deny us that.

I taste her lower lip, grazing it with my teeth, and she opens up for me. I sink my tongue into the sweetness of her mouth and groan.

She is perfect.

Her plump lips mold to mine like they are made for each other, and when her slim fingers grab my t-shirt and drag me toward her, I wrap one arm around her waist and the other hand around the back of her neck.

She moans softly, pushing her chest against mine, arching her back, molding every curve against my body. She drives me crazy. Every single cell of my skin is on high alert and taking in her touch, her heat, her presence.

I kiss her slowly, taking my time tasting her, smelling her skin, and enjoying her touch. When I pull back to catch my breath, she whimpers in protest and slowly opens her eyes. I'm not ready to see the molten desire filling her gaze.

I grab the back of her thighs and lift her onto the kitchen counter, nestling myself between her legs. My erection presses against the thin layer of fabric of her shorts, and I'm not sure I can stop at a kiss.

I graze her lips with mine, and when she grabs a fistful of hair between her fingers, I'm almost sure I'll lose it. I clasp her hips with my hands, enjoying the softness of her thighs, and then I sink my tongue in her mouth and push my erection against her core. She moans, and I swallow every single one of those sounds, never leaving her lips, her mouth, her unmistakable desire.

When she catches her breath, I lower my forehead to hers. "So? Did you like this one?" I ask. My voice comes out deep and rough.

"Yes!" She breathes out.

"Perfect, because I liked it too. A lot," I say, pushing away from the counter.

"Perfect." She grins but then frowns when I turn around, grab the plate from the microwave and start to walk away.

"Hey! Are you just going to leave me like this?" She asks, wide-eyed.

I wink at her and grin but keep walking to my room. I'm ready for a kiss, and my body is pushing for a lot more, but my mind and my heart are still too tender to jump into something like that so soon.

Wendy Ashford—The grump and the chef

# Chapter 11

It's been fifteen days since the last earth-shattering kiss I shared with Noah. A kiss that still makes me dream of his lips on mine, his demanding tongue, and his possessive hands on my hips. And his massive erection pressed against my core? *That* is something I will never forget. That man is pure perfection, masculinity, and disarming sweetness.

The problem is that there's been nothing after those two magnificent kisses. He hasn't made one move to look for more. And I don't get it. I mean, I know he liked it, so why not explore the attraction? He told me he's no longer hung up on his ex, and I believe him. But why not have some fun?

I watch him while he washes the dishes, his muscles straining under that t-shirt, his perfect ass wrapped in those too-tight gray sweatpants. They shouldn't sell that kind of pants to men. They should be illegal. Aren't there women in the marketing departments going absolutely insane at the photos in the ad campaigns for these things? I mean, it's pretty obvious when a man puts on gray sweatpants, every woman's brain within a one-mile radius literally becomes possessed, a hostage of their own hormones.

"Are you checking me out?" Noah's deep voice startles me.

I raise my gaze to his face and see a big fat smirk under that sexy beard. I imagine tickling it, and not just with my mouth but with a lot of other body parts.

"What? No!" I protest.

"Yes, you were. I caught you staring at my ass." That damn smirk never leaves his face.

"You wish," I scoff. "I was watching how carefully you wash those dishes. You're particularly careful with the pans." I have no idea what the heck I'm saying.

He crosses his arms and those spectacular biceps bulge. *Please, don't do that, Noah. I'm trying not to drool over here!*

"From where you're sitting on the counter, all you can see is my back, not how I'm doing the dishes. Oh, and clearly my ass." Now he's teasing me.

I stiffen my back and train my face into a neutral expression. "Well, it's not my fault. It's your sweatpants' fault."

He looks down at his pants, which clearly outline the bulge between his legs. "What's wrong with my sweatpants?" He sounds genuinely puzzled.

"Oh, for fuck's sake, Noah! Everyone knows that gray sweatpants are like kryptonite for every woman on earth. You can't go around flaunting those pants and not expect me to drool all over you. I can't even control my saliva when you wear those. I'm like a Great Dane in front of a food bowl!" I complain, and his eyes widen.

He stares at me for a long time, and then he shakes his head. "You know you're crazy, right?"

"No, I'm not. Everyone knows that. Like, they teach it in college: The great threat of the gray sweatpants."

He struggles not to laugh. "And by the way, you are not a Great Dane in this whole conspiracy story. Considering your size and attitude, you're more of a Chihuahua. Always freezing cold under thousands of blankets and incapable of keeping your mouth shut!" he teases with a grin.

"I am not!" Now I'm really offended. I never liked those dogs, especially when they try to bite me.

Noah laughs and shakes his head. "Yes, you are. Look at what you're wearing right now."

I look down at my two sweaters and thick fleece leggings. When I packed to come here, I didn't plan to stay for months, especially not with a man. A hot one. One I'd think about taking off these clothes for. I didn't pack anything nice I would wear on a date. And the thought that I'd even consider living here a date is crazy proof that this situation is driving me nuts.

"Well, I was going to change!" I say stubbornly, standing up and walking to my suitcase in a corner of the living room.

Noah follows my every movement with amusement. I drag the suitcase into the bathroom and open it. Not a lot to work with, but if Noah thinks he has me figured out, he's mistaken. I'll put him in the same hormonal instability I'm in right now and see if he's still laughing. I mean, maybe he'll decide another kiss isn't such a bad idea after all. I smile, grabbing a T-shirt and the shorts I wear for sleep in New York but not here because they're a bit too tight to walk around in a stranger's house. But considering I was kissing *that stranger* a couple of weeks ago, why not?

I put on my t-shirt, deciding to ditch my bra and pull on the skimpy shorts. Well, it's freaking cold, so my nipples are poking through the thin layer of fabric. I have no idea how Noah can go around the house in just a t-shirt. Okay, the fireplace does have a system of pipes that runs under the floor and connects with a hot water heater that basically heats this entire cabin—a very cool feature Noah was proud to explain to me. But it's snowing outside! When it snows, you put on sweaters, no matter how hot it is in the house.

When I finally come out of the bathroom, Noah is sitting in his armchair reading a book. I've never met a guy who reads so much, and I admit, Noah is even sexy doing that. I sit on the couch and grab a novel out

of my pile. Jack takes a spot next to me and rests his head on my legs.

"What the hell are you wearing?" Noah asks me, puzzled, putting down his book.

"What? Something comfortable, like you." I play dumb.

He shakes his head and tries, failing, not to stare at the tight shorts that wrap around my butt.

"I'm not equipped if you catch pneumonia. You know that, right?" He lowers his eyes again on the book, but I catch him skimming his heated gaze over my body.

"I'm not cold." I'm totally lying, and my nipples are ratting me out.

Noah lowers his eyes to see them poking through the t-shirt, a smirk forming on his lips. "Are you sure about that?"

I scoff, but I can't answer without feeling my face going up in flames. Okay, maybe I didn't think through this one. I admit my plan is a bit faulty, but I'm too proud to back down, and I go back to reading my book.

"Why aren't you reading?" Noah asks after a while.

"I am reading!" Not sure what, but I'm doing it.

"No, you're not. You've been staring at the same page for fifteen minutes," he points out, and he's right.

"Are you checking if I'm reading or not? You're like a third-grade teacher, checking what the kids are doing during reading time." I lower my book.

Noah puts down his biography, too, and sighs. "I'm not checking, but you keep huffing so loudly it's distracting. You do it when you're bored," he states matter-of-factly.

"I am bored," I admit, whining.

"You have a pile of books. Why aren't you reading?"

He seems genuinely surprised I can't find the strength to do it. "I'm more of a mood reader," I explain.

Noah frowns and looks at me like I'm crazy. "A what?"

"A mood reader. I read books based on my mood. One day, I can be obsessed with an epic fantasy, and the next day, I need an urban fantasy romance. Sometimes, something happens in the middle of the book that sets my mood off, and I need to change."

Noah looks close to freaking out. "You have literally eight books over there. Do you have more than eight moods?" He clearly thinks I'm schizophrenic. I can read it all over his face.

"No! They're all part of the same series. That's just one mood!" I explain, and his eyes grow wide.

"Wait. Let me get this straight." He leans closer to the piles of books. "You bought an entire series without reading the first book to know if you like it?"

Putting it like that sounds a bit insane, I admit. But I really thought I was going to love this series. "Yeah.

Sometimes, I get super hyped about a series and then struggle through the first book," I admit and feel my cheeks heat up.

"You are completely crazy, you know that?"

"I am not! I'm just prepared. If I really like the series, I can read all the books without waiting to buy the next one."

"But now you're bored because you have a series you don't want to read." He's always so logical it's almost frustrating.

"Can we play poker?" I whine. Not my best behavior, but I'm really bored out of my mind in here.

Noah closes his book and puts it on the coffee table. "Sometimes you make me want to burn down this entire cabin." He sighs but stands up and grabs the deck of cards.

I put a pillow on the floor near the fireplace, in front of the coffee table, and sit there. Jack complains a bit but then jumps down from the couch and curls up on his bed next to the fireplace.

"Let's make this interesting," I suggest. "Instead of answering questions, the loser has to do a dare."

Noah shakes his head and smiles. "How old are you? Twelve?"

"Oh, come on! Do you always play by the rules? What do you care if we're twelve or thirty? It's not like we'd do something stupid. Or are you afraid of what I might dare you to do?" I challenge him.

He shuffles the cards and gives me my hand. "Considering how crazy you are, yes, I'm afraid."

At least he's honest. "I promise I won't ask you to do something dangerous."

"Okay, let's just get on with it."

Exactly five minutes later, I think he's regretting agreeing with me. He loses the first round, and he's already starting to protest about the rules when I beat him to it.

"I dare you to kiss me." A smug smile on my face is not enough to cancel Noah's raised eyebrow.

He opens his mouth once, twice, but says nothing. He seems to think about it, evaluating the pros and cons. I'm almost sure he'll back out when he grabs my hand and drags me to him. I'm pressed against his chest, and the heat in his eyes is almost animalistic.

His hands tug at the thin fabric of my shorts, and he drags me to straddle him. Suddenly, those gray sweatpants are too much in the way. He stares at me for a long, heated moment, then grabs my hair in a fist and crushes his mouth on mine.

His beard tickles my lips, but when I open them for him, his tongue sweeps away my every thought— tickling or anything else that could distract me. When Noah kisses you, you become part of his world and all of the heated passion he puts into it.

One hand tightens around my hair, and the other explores the hem of my shorts. A moan escapes my

Wendy Ashford—The grump and the chef

lips when he explores close, so close, to my core, and I'm pretty sure he can feel the dampness between my thighs.

The sound seems to trigger a groan that rumbles in his chest. I can feel it on my breasts, pressed against his hard pecs. I can feel it on my fingers that are exploring the muscles on his back. It's so intense and animalistic that I thank God I'm straddling his lap because my legs would give out.

Before his lips leave mine, he bites my lower lip, sucking a bit, pulling another moan from my throat. When I finally look Noah in the eyes, the storm sweeping those green irises is breathtaking. I've never seen such passion in a man's gaze. It's almost like he wants to devour every inch of my skin, and I know I'll love every single second of it.

He tightens his grip on my hair and presses me closer to the erection awakening in his pants. I'm almost sure he's going to kiss me. His gaze focuses on my swollen lips. He bites his lower lip. But when an impatient whimper escapes my throat, his eyes snap to mine and widen. Suddenly, all the magic is lost, like a cold bucket of ice has been dumped on our heads.

He eases me down off his lap and stands up so abruptly that the coffee table almost topples over. He turns around and stalks toward the back door that leads to the garage.

"Where are you going?" I ask breathlessly, partly because of the kiss, partly because of the sudden change of mood.

"I'm going to fix the snowmobile," he mumbles loud enough for me to hear.

"What the hell?" I say as he closes the door behind him.

Jack comes closer, sits on the floor next to me, and puts his head on my legs. I stare at the door for a long time, not sure if I should follow him and ask for an explanation. I'm starting to hate that snowmobile. I'm glad he decided to take a look at it—it's safer if he can get to town if he needs to—but I also know he's doing it to kick me out of his place.

Every day he spends in the garage is a day closer to me leaving this cozy cabin. And the more I think about it, the more I'm not sure I want to go back. Returning to New York means I have to face the fact that I don't know what to do with my life. My dream to open a restaurant is just that, a dream, and I have to deal with the reality that I'm jobless, homeless, and my stuff is stacked in boxes in a storage unit.

And that freaking kiss! How could I leave a man whose kisses leave me so breathless?

Wendy Ashford—The grump and the chef

# Chapter 12

I am an idiot. I want her. There's no doubt I want to worship every inch of her body. And even though she's annoying most of the time, I like having her around. She's smart and curious. I love how she gasps when I explain something she doesn't know and the passion she pours into teaching me how to cook her favorite recipes.

She's intelligent, funny, and hot. So damn hot.

Those kisses have driven me insane since the first time I tasted her. God only knows how many times I've woken up during the night and had to take care of my erection because there weren't enough gruesome thoughts in the world to get rid of it.

So why am I here, staring at a snowmobile I'm not fixing instead of burying myself between her thighs? Because I'm an idiot, that's why. She'll break me just like I was broken ten years ago. Or not. There's no way of knowing.

I put down the rag I'm holding and go to the sink to wash the grease stains off my hands. I've been working for the last two hours without really fixing this thing. Damn, I'm so distracted I should probably double-check what I did today.

I take a deep breath, and after drying my hands, I walk back inside to apologize to her. I owe her an apology for how I treated her. For how I kissed her and then left her there without an explanation. Again. But when I walk into the kitchen, my every thought is completely erased by the view in front of me.

Olivia is bent at the waist, checking something she's baking in the oven. Her ass is on full display in those tiny shorts, and I can see the line of the fabric creeping up between her butt cheeks. It's a vision to die for. My cock twitches in my pants. *I know, buddy. I know!*

She stands up and turns around, startled, squealing when she sees me. "What the hell are you doing here staring like a creeper?" She puts a hand over her heart to still it.

"Sorry, didn't mean to scare you with your head stuck in the oven." *And yes, I was staring at your ass.*

She frowns for a moment, but then a smile crosses her face. At least she doesn't seem upset about my behavior this morning. "I'm making my famous sweet raisin bread." She beams.

I frown. "Where did you find the raisins?" I don't remember buying them.

She rolls her eyes. "Well, I couldn't find any, so I used dried plums."

I laugh. "Okay, good. I'm glad you didn't use something that's probably been there for years."

She makes a face. "Do I look like someone who uses expired ingredients?"

No, she's someone who can bake anything from scratch.

"Listen," she starts seriously. "I wasn't trying to push you into something you didn't want before. Sorry I asked you to kiss me. I thought you liked it. I misunderstood." She sounds almost shy.

I look at her for a long while, dumbfounded. It takes me that long to realize she's apologizing to me. It should be the other way around.

"Stop. You don't have to apologize. You did nothing wrong. I just don't know how to navigate this stuff between us. It's confusing. I'm confused, and I…" I stop because I realize I'm not confused at all. Scared of being hurt again? Yes. Confused if I want her or not? Hell no! I'm not confused at all, I want her. Full stop.

"So, you're not mad because I kissed you?" She tilts her head, frowning like she always does when she can't figure out something, and that sweet, confused expression makes me snap.

I grab a fistful of her hair from the back of her neck and drag her luscious body against mine. She widens her eyes before I crush my lips on hers and kiss the hell out of her. She opens for me like she was waiting for forever, and when my tongue meets hers, a small moan escapes her lips. God, I love those moans and whimpers she makes when she's turned on.

Her hands grab my t-shirt and pull it like I'm a tree she wants to climb. I tighten my embrace around her waist and press her against my chest. I love feeling her soft curves against my body. She's small; I have to bend down a bit to reach her, but she arches her back to mold her body to mine.

When I pull back from her, we're both panting.

"You definitely didn't misunderstand the situation," I say, out of breath.

"I had my suspicions," she giggles, a sound I didn't know could turn me on.

She sneaks her hands under the hem of my t-shirt, and a shiver runs down my spine. My skin tingles under her touch.

"If you don't stop that, I won't stop kissing you," I warn her. My voice is raspy with pleasure.

"Who says I want you to stop?" she breathes, and I'm done.

I look into her eyes, searching for any sign of doubt or uncertainty, but I find only lust. I reluctantly leave my hands from her body and play with the hem of her shirt. She stops me, and my heart sinks. Maybe she's not so sure about this new development, but then she grabs my t-shirt and pulls it up.

Wendy Ashford—The grump and the chef

"You first," she orders, wide-eyed.

I help her tear off the fabric covering my upper body, happy to see the awe in her eyes. I know I'm not bad looking, but her eyes devouring me like I'm a fucking meal is a view I can get used to. She puts her hands on my pecs and caresses me lightly, playing with the short hair dusting my chest. She leans closer and kisses first my right pec, then the left. The soft, torturous touch of her lips makes me groan in pleasure.

I watch her looking up at me with a mischievous smile on her lips, and when she flicks her tongue over my nipple, I almost come in my pants like a teenager his first time.

"Fuck! Are you trying to kill me?" My voice is raspy and full of lust I can't contain.

"Why? Don't you like it?" she asks innocently before putting her mouth on my left nipple and sucking it, teasing me with her tongue.

"Fuck!" That's my only reply. Not the most clever, but a guttural one for sure.

I grab a fistful of her hair while she keeps switching from my left to right nipple. I didn't know that could be so erotic. Now I know why women go crazy when I do it. I've never been with someone who pays this much attention to me, maybe because I've always looked for a quick fuck with the least amount of fuss.

Her hands travel along my abs like she's trying to commit my body to memory. I'm so turned on that if I

don't bury myself in her soon, I'll likely die. But when I reach for her shirt, she goes stiff.

"If you don't want to do it, tell me. We can stop any-time." I frown at her shy gaze. I'll probably need to run outside naked to smother my erection, but I'd never force myself on a woman, no matter how horny I am.

"It's not like I don't want to, but..." she mumbles, embarrassment coloring her cheeks.

"But what? You don't have to have sex just be-cause you think I want to." I don't get what's holding her back. She seems turned on but embarrassed about something.

"Don't you want me to keep my shirt on?" she blurts out without looking me in the eye.

I'm stunned by her question. It's not like she's ashamed of sex. I mean, she talks a lot about it and makes fun of me sometimes. "Why on earth would I want that?" I frown.

"I don't know. I'm not exactly a supermodel, and my boobs…you know…shake like pudding when I move. And my belly too. Let's not even talk about my thighs!" she tries to explain, but all I can focus on is that someone made her think she's ugly because she has curves.

I tip her chin, forcing her to look into my eyes. "I don't know if you've noticed, but everything about you turns me on. From your spectacular boobs to your glorious ass. I'm rock hard right now, just seeing you

Wendy Ashford—The grump and the chef

bend in front of the oven with your butt begging to be fucked. I want to see everything about you, I want to worship your body like the goddess you are." Her eyes widen like she can't believe I'm saying these words. "I don't know who asked you to cover up during sex, but he doesn't deserve someone like you. He's an idiot."

She smiles and nods. "So, you were staring at my ass."

I burst out laughing. "Yes. I was drooling over it."

She seems pleased at my confession, and when she grabs the hem of her t-shirt and pulls it over her head, my mouth goes dry.

"Fuck," I breathe when I see those perfect, glorious tits with two dusk-pink nipples reclaiming my attention. I fall on my knees, grab her by the hips and drag her to me. I kiss and bite her soft, perfect, belly, getting a giggle from her, but when I focus on those beautiful boobs, her giggles become moans.

She buries her fingers in my hair while I palm her breasts and lean in to suck a nipple. A whimper escapes her lips when I bite delicately on the peak. I look up and find her with her eyes closed, lips parted, and her head tilted back. She is gorgeous.

Her grip on my hair tightens when I lick and suck on her nipple, slightly pinching the other one between my fingers. She whimpers in response, and I almost come when she pushes her breast against my face, demanding more. I grab her full boobs and squeeze a bit.

They're big enough to fill my hands and then some. God, she is a dream.

I keep sucking on her nipple and sneak a hand between her legs. Her shorts are soaked. I tease her a bit with my fingers, caressing lightly over the thin fabric, and she starts to rock her hips, trying to ride my hand. When I move my fingers away, she huffs in protest, but then stiffens a bit when I put my fingers under the elastic band of her shorts and start to pull down.

I stop, not sure about her reaction, and look up. She's biting her lower lip and looking at me like she can't wait to sink her teeth into a succulent bite of food. I've never seen so much desire in someone, especially not for me. She looks like she's never experienced someone wanting to fuck her senseless, and I can't understand how that's even possible.

I slowly lower her panties, never leaving her eyes. She stares at me with a mischievous smile as she steps out of her shorts. I guide her toward the kitchen counter, where she leans back, and then I sink my face between her thighs. She catches her breath, biting her lower lip. A moan escapes her throat when I lick my way over her wet opening. She tastes sweet, and I close my eyes for a moment, enjoying her perfect, warm body.

I repeat the slow flick of my tongue, and she chokes out a "fuck" that gets lost in the moan that follows. I grab her firm ass and drag her sweet pussy against my mouth, sucking and licking her juices. She puts her el-

Wendy Ashford—The grump and the chef

bows on the counter behind her to hold herself better, and I lift her legs, one after the other, over my shoulders, her ass still squeezed between my fingers.

I stick my tongue between her wet folds and suck greedily. God, she is perfect when she rides my face. I lap a few more times, and then I focus on that sweet spot where her thighs meet. Her clit is red and swollen, ready to take on the assault of my tongue. She cries out loud when I take the bundle of nerves in my mouth and suck hard while slipping a couple of fingers inside her. She's so wet they meet no resistance, even as she tightens around my knuckles. I suck a little more and bend my fingers to reach that silky spot inside her that I hope will drive her crazy. And there it is. She comes apart, clenching around my fingers with a loud growl shaking her chest.

"Sweet Jesus," she breathes out, trying to catch her breath.

I help put her feet down and catch her when her legs give out. She kneels in front of me, all flushed and beautiful. Her hair is a mess, her cheeks pink, and I've never seen someone so gorgeous.

She leans in and kisses me with a passion that consumes us both. Every stroke of her tongue is a jolt straight to my cock. My cock, craving to be buried deep inside her. And…

"Fuck! I don't have a condom." My heart sinks, and my dick almost hurts in protest.

She looks me in the eyes and smiles. "I'm clean. I got tested a few weeks before I got here and haven't had sex since. If you're tested regularly, I don't think we need one."

"I'm clean too. I get tested every year before coming up here for the winter, and it's not like I have a lot of women coming and going during winter. I'm more worried about a pregnancy." I wince. Not exactly the conversation I imagined after going down on her, with my cock ready to fall off if it doesn't get some action.

"I have an IUD. I'm safe from pregnancy for the next eight years. Do you think you can manage to fuck me before it expires?"

I burst out laughing. "Trust me, at the risk of sounding like a loser, you're so gorgeous I won't last more than fifteen minutes."

She laughs, too, and pushes me onto the warm floor. They told me I was crazy to put all that effort into this heating system for a small wooden cabin. Well, who's having the best sex of his life without freezing to death now?

Olivia helps me out of my sweatpants, and her eyes bulge when my erection springs free.

"Holy shit!" Her mouth hangs open. "I imagined you were packed down there, but I underestimated your manhood."

Her statement is so bold and honest I can't help but laugh. I reach out my hand, drag her to me, and kiss her

146

until we can't catch our breath. She kisses my lips, my jaw, moving down my neck and chest. She takes her time on my nipples, making me growl in appreciation. She tastes each ab muscle before kissing her way down to my cock. She looks me straight in the eyes, grinning before licking my shaft, balls to tip, and then sinking my cock deep in her throat.

"Fuck!" the word catches in my chest because I can't breathe. She is a fucking goddess.

She frees my dick from her luscious lips with a loud pop, and then swirls her tongue around the tip before sucking it into her mouth again. I have no idea where she learned something like that, but I want to kiss the guy who taught it to her.

"If you keep at this, I'll come in your mouth," I manage to rasp without losing it.

"And you don't want to?" She pouts. Damn! I almost tell her to keep going.

"Another time, yes, but right now, I want to sink balls deep into that glorious pussy."

She smiles and starts to crawl up my body until she straddles my hips. She looks me straight in the eyes as she positions my cock underneath her opening and lowers, slowly sinking my shaft in her warm slick pussy. I'm going to lose this battle with my body.

She starts to ride me, rolling her hips slowly, putting her hands on my pecs, and pushing down until I fill her completely. I knew she would be tight. I didn't know how tight. I'm going to come in record time.

She keeps a steady pace, rising up until my cock almost spills out, then sinking down again, with an exasperated groan from me. I let her hips dictate the rhythm and put my hands on her glorious tits. She whimpers when I squeeze them, raising my head to suck her nipples. When I bite the hard peaks, she picks up the speed and starts to ride me harder, chasing her orgasm like it's a race she wants to win.

I meet her strokes, pushing up my hips, and when she comes clenching around my cock, the only thing I can do is ride the waves of my own orgasm, filling her up with my seed. I can't control it, and it's so intense I can hear the blood pumping in my veins and…bells. I hear bells. Not in a figurative way, but like some kind of mystic orgasmic experience.

"What the hell is that noise?" I ask when she collapses in my arms, kissing my chest and panting like she can't get enough oxygen in her lungs.

She starts to laugh, shaking while I keep her in a tight hug. "It's the timer. I have to take the bread out of the oven."

I laugh too. "Shit. I thought I was hearing things. I mean, that was the best sex of my life, but hearing bells is a bit strange even for this."

"Best sex of your life, huh?" She looks at me with a smug smile.

Wendy Ashford—The grump and the chef

I think about it, and yes. That was the best sex I've ever had. Because it's not some meaningless act with a stranger I picked up at a bar. Fuck.

# Chapter 13

I wake up smiling blissfully when I realize I'm snuggled against Noah's hard chest. His arms are wrapped around me, our naked bodies cocooned in the warm blanket.

Yesterday, it was like a dam bursting open. Once we got to the hot part, we couldn't stop. We did it in the kitchen, twice. And in the bedroom three times. Who knew a man could keep up with all that? Not that I'm too surprised. Noah is built like a truck; it doesn't take a genius to figure out he has a lot of stamina.

I'm so sore, I don't even know if I can walk today. Fortunately, another storm is raging outside right now, so we don't have to do anything but wait for spring. The idea that I can't go back to New York is not as bad as it was at first. I should be worried about everything happening at home while I'm stuck here, but the reality is, I'm stuck here. I can't do anything to change it, so why not enjoy it?

"Good morning." Noah's rough voice make his chest rumble under my head.

"Good morning." I kiss his pec as he tightens his arms around me.

His morning wood is pressed against my stomach. His hard, massive erection I thought was going to split me in half, but instead gave me an earthshattering orgasm—or eight. I hook a leg over his hip, and he groans.

"If you keep rubbing against me like that, I'm going to fuck you before I even open my eyes." His deep raspy voice sends a pleasant shiver down my body and my pussy clenches despite the soreness. I chuckle when he strokes his shaft against my belly.

"I want to, but I really need to use the bathroom."

He groans disappointedly when I slip out of his grasp and stand up, putting on my t-shirt and the shorts I wore yesterday.

"You'll kill me if you keep wearing those panties." He chuckles, opening his eyes, putting his hands behind his head, and staring at my butt.

"You seemed very alive yesterday," I point out with a smug smile.

"Because I took them off before I dropped dead."

I laugh, grabbing the door handle and walking out of the room.

When I close the bathroom door behind me, a sense of unease invades me. Yesterday, we were caught in the frenzy of the moment. But what happens when I walk out of here? Will it be awkward? Do we pretend this never happened or that this is our new normal? I know Noah doesn't do dating. Heck, he lives like a hermit up here. Saying he doesn't date is the understatement of the century.

What if he feels uncomfortable because we're stuck together, and he doesn't want anything to do with me after tonight? The truth is, I have no idea what will happen next, and I tend to be overdramatic when it comes to relationships. I'm always trying to guess what the other person wants and, eventually, make things easy and leave if I don't feel welcome. But I can't leave this time. I have to face the awkwardness and deal with it. I've never missed Ava so much in my life. Only she can talk me down from these crazy ledges.

"Are you okay in there?" Noah's worried voice comes through the door.

I hadn't noticed how much time had passed while I was overthinking. I take a deep breath, wash my hands, and walk out before I have a full meltdown. I find Noah downstairs in the kitchen cooking breakfast. He's wearing those damn gray sweatpants and nothing else. I can't help but stare at those drool-worthy muscles flexing as he uses the spatula.

When he notices me staring, he smiles, grabs my wrist, and drags me to him. He cages me against the stove, my back against his chest. With one hand, he



Wendy Ashford—The grump and the chef

keeps stirring the eggs; with the other, he circles my waist. His chin is resting on my head, and from time to time, he kisses my cheeks.

Okay. I suppose all the worry was just in my head. Noah seems fine with continuing where we left off last night.

"Why can I hear you thinking?" he asks me after a bit of silence.

"I'm not thinking." Dumb answer, I know.

He chuckles. "Yes, you are. You normally drive me crazy with your chatter. You keep your mouth shut only when you're overthinking."

Did he notice that? "I didn't know what would happen between us when I came out of that bathroom."

"What do you mean?" He tightens his grip on my waist.

"I don't know. I thought maybe it would be awkward if you didn't like what we did yesterday," I confess.

The truth is, I was naked, completely and utterly naked. Greg always asked me to cover up because my extra fat was distracting for him during sex. What if Noah realized that too? Maybe the first time he was too horny, but the fifth he took his time to look at me. Really look at me while he licked every inch of my body.

"And it took me five mind-blowing orgasms to come to that conclusion?" he grumbles against my ear while he nips at my lobe.



The grump and the chef—Wendy Ashford

A small moan escapes my lips. It's not fair to distract me with the prelude of sex while I'm overthinking! "Are you sure you don't want me to cover up when we do it?" I didn't mean to say it out loud, but when he's nipping at my skin, sending pleasure all through my body, I can't think straight enough to filter what I say.

He goes still behind me. He turns off the stove and grips my hips, turning me around. I put my hands on his hips and look him in the eyes.

He's frowning, and I see some anger, maybe, in the downward curve of his lips. "I don't know who convinced you that skinny is the standard of beauty, but you have to stop thinking that every man likes a skinny woman. I love your curves. I love getting lost in the softness of your body. If I die suffocated by your glorious tits or your fantastic ass, I will die with a smile on my face."

A smile forms on my lips. "Okay. I trust you." And I do because I can't see a trace of a lie on his face. I laugh when he arches an eyebrow and pushes his hips against my belly, making it clear that even his erection agrees with him. I've never had a man get a constant hard-on when he's around me.

He kisses my forehead, then grabs two plates, puts the breakfast on them, and turns around to sit at the kitchen counter.

"Are you working on the snowmobile today?" I ask, sitting next to him and digging into my breakfast.

Wendy Ashford—The grump and the chef

He shrugs his shoulders and shakes his head. "I don't know. I have to figure out how to fix it because I don't have a spare part I need. I know there's a work-around, but I don't know what it is yet."

"I have the solution for you." I smile when his eyebrow arches in a doubtful expression.

"I'm afraid to ask," he mumbles.

"Yoga. You should do yoga and free your mind from every thought. It helps me every time I'm stuck with something," I gingerly propose, and he shakes his head.

"I knew I should have been afraid," he breathes out.

***

The yoga session goes like every other time we try and do it together. Rooster is perched on the back of the couch, staring at us, Jack is trying to imitate our poses and getting in the way, and Noah complains about everything I make him do. This time, he has a reason to complain because I admit I'm doing some difficult poses for a beginner, but his butt is such a dream to look at in those close-fitting gray sweatpants.

Noah grunts for the umpteenth time and sits on the floor next to me. Jack jumps toward him to lick his face.

"I've had enough of this torture. Forty-five minutes, and I'm sweating like a pig," he complains, drying his forehead with a towel.

His chest is glistering with perspiration and I want to run my hands all over it. Just to dry his skin, of course. "It's good for your health," I counter, sitting down next to him and sipping from my water bottle.

"I can think about other, more pleasurable, activities that make me sweat," he says with a smug smile on his face.

"Really? Any suggestion?" I ask, and my lower belly is already tingling in anticipation.

"Why don't we talk about it under the shower?" he suggests, helping me stand up and pushing me toward the bathroom.

As soon as he closes the door behind us, Noah presses his chest against my back, pushing me against the sink. He grins at me in the mirror while he grabs my t-shirt and pulls it over my head, leaving my breasts naked in front of him. He grabs them from behind and kneads them like there's nothing else he'd rather do for the rest of his life. He plays with my already hardening nipples, enjoying every single moan that escapes my throat.

I close my eyes and lean my head on his chest, pushing my ass against his erection. He growls when I dry hump him, pushing me harder against the sink. He lowers himself and nibbles at my neck, tickling me with his thick beard.

Noah slides his hands down my hips, puts a couple of fingers under the waistband of my panties, and drags

Wendy Ashford—The grump and the chef

them down my legs, leaving me completely naked. I open my eyes and stare at him in the mirror while he gets rid of his sweatpants without ever breaking eye contact. I love the contrast between our two sizes. I'm not as thin as most girls I know, but he's huge compared to me. He makes me feel small in his arms, protected.

He turns around to turn on the shower, putting a hand in it to feel the temperature, and when it's finally hot enough, he beckons me to follow him under the water. I expect him to push me against the wall and fuck me with the same passion as last night, but he surprises me by grabbing the soap and lathering his hands before turning me around and soaping up my shoulders, my arms, then going down to my breasts and focusing on them. When this shower is over, they'll be clean. Thoroughly clean.

He plays with my breasts for a long time while rubbing against my back with his erection, and when his hands focus on the lower part of my abdomen, my pussy clenches in anticipation. His thick fingers play in circles over my clit, sliding periodically between my folds. I'm so aroused I think he could penetrate me in one thrust, and I'd be okay with it.

Noah wraps a hand around my waist, and slips a couple of fingers inside me, making me groan with pleasure.

"Keep it up and I'll come so fast you won't even know it happened," I pant.

Noah chuckles and bites my shoulder gently. "Really? I'm just washing you. You're so dirty down here," he growls in my ear, pushing his fingers deeper inside me.

I cry out. "Oh, yes. I'm filthy. Keep going!"

His chest presses against my back, shaking with a chuckle, and when he pulls his fingers out, I whimper in protest. He slips his hand further back, reaching between my butt cheeks, teasing the other hole back there. I tense a bit. I'm not used to opening up my back door, but Noah gently coaxes my muscles to relax and slips the tip of his finger in. It's a strange sensation, but I'm so turned on it's not completely unpleasant.

When he turns me around and starts to rinse me, I frown. "What are you doing?" My voice is shaken by the sudden change.

Noah grins at me but doesn't stop. "I'm washing you. What did you think I was doing?"

My mouth hangs open. "Are you serious?"

"Of course," he teases me.

I look at him for a long time, trying to figure out if he's kidding, but when he keeps cleaning the soap from my boobs, I drop to my knees and stare back at his lust-covered face. If he wants war, I'm ready to fight back.

I look him straight in the eyes, challenging him to stop me, as I wrap my lips around his throbbing erection and let it slide deep down my throat.

Wendy Ashford—The grump and the chef

"Fuck!" he whispers under his breath when I start to bob my head.

I grab the base of his shaft in a firm grip and mimic the movement of my head. He puts his hands on the wall in front of him and lowers his head, watching me and breathing hard. The hot water cascades over his shoulders, washing down in rivulets over his chiseled chest.

I let his erection out of my mouth with a loud pop before licking my way down from the tip to his balls. I gently wrap my lips around one and suck lightly. The "fuck" that growls out of his chest is almost animalistic. I suck a little harder, and he closes his eyes, breathing hard, fisting his hands against the wall. His abs tense, and when I slowly lick my way up to his tip, he pushes his hips forward, sinking his erection between my lips. He puts a hand on the back of my head and fucks my mouth slowly. I reach down with my fingers between my legs and circle my clit slowly, following his rhythm. I moan when the orgasm starts to mount again.

"I don't want to come in your mouth," he whispers, helping me to my feet.

His lips crush mine as he tastes me with a soft moan, and I wrap my arms around his neck. He grabs my thighs and lifts me against the wall like I weigh nothing. I wrap my legs around his hips, and when he sinks deep inside of me, he finds no resistance. He fills me to the brim, and the feeling is so amazing I cry out, biting his shoulder.

He fucks me hard against the wall, each stroke hitting that spot inside me that makes my legs tremble. We come together in a bliss of pleasure and groans.

The storm is still raging outside, and I'm happy I can't go home.

Wendy Ashford—The grump and the chef

# Chapter 14

I wake up with Olivia's head resting on my chest. She snores slightly and, from the cold sensation on my skin, I think she's drooling. I smile. We had sex for the first time three days ago and never stopped. I've postponed a lot of work I usually do around the house to keep myself busy. Small things, nothing major, like reorganizing and cleaning the cabinets in the kitchen or doing my laundry.

It's something I do regularly, to keep me occupied while I wait for spring to come. There was a year at the beginning when I didn't come out of my room for days. I was a mess and being trapped up here didn't help. I thought I was going crazy, thinking about my ex and drowning in self-pity. That year, I reached rock bottom and from then on, I forced myself to stay busy. Always get out of bed, always find things to do.

If I knew I could spend my days having sex with a woman, I would have considered living with some-



The grump and the chef—Wendy Ashford

one way sooner. The thought leaves a bitter taste in my mouth. I'm not living with Olivia. She's trapped here by accident, and we're doing our best to survive until spring. She's not going to stay once the snow melts.

I look down at her messy blond mane and watch her stir. I was right, she is drooling. I smile. She opens one eye, cleans her mouth with the back of her hand, and makes a disgusted face when she realizes it's wet. I chuckle, getting her attention.

"Sorry about that," she groggily apologizes, cleaning my chest with the corner of the sheet.

"It's okay. After what we did in this bed, I'm not worried about a bit of saliva." I kiss her head.

She blushes furiously. We're probably thinking the same thing: how I used her tits last night to get off and came all over her neck and face. It was the hottest sex I had ever had. I like how she's willing to experiment between the sheets, and I'm also glad she lost her discomfort with getting naked in front of me. Her ex should be behind the bars for making her feel inadequate.

She bites my nipple lightly, and I shiver. "I need a shower. My hair is sticky and I stink."

"Your hair is a mess, but you don't stink." I can feel my erection awakening just having her pressed against me. If I don't do something, I'll end up fucking her brains out again without leaving this room for yet another day.

Wendy Ashford—The grump and the chef

"Now you're just being nice." She pats my chest before sitting up.

"Go take a shower and fix some breakfast. I'm going out to get a surprise ready for you." I wink at her when her face lights up with a smile.

"Really? What is it?" She's like a child at Christmas.

"Are you aware of the concept of surprise?" I raise my inquisitive eyebrow. "You know, where I don't tell you what it is and you gasp when you see it with your own eyes?"

She rolls her eyes and puts on my t-shirt. It's a natural gesture, I don't think she even notices she grabbed it, but it settles strangely in my chest. I like seeing her in my clothes. I feel like she belongs to me, and that thought scares me.

"Okay. I just hope it's not a five-mile trek in the middle of the storm." She nails me to the bed with a glare.

"Can you hear it?" I ask.

She frowns. "What. I can't hear anything."

"Exactly! The storm stopped last night."

She smiles and reaches for the door. "Are you sure you don't want to come shower with me?" Her voice drips sensuality.

I'm tempted to give up my plans and fuck her against the shower wall, but I resist the urge to sink my dick between her thighs. I put my hands behind my head, leaving my chest naked, my erection tenting under the sheets, and I smirk.

"Damn! You are not telling me what the surprise is, are you?" she complains.

"Nope."

She walks out, muttering something I can't make out, and I sit up, ready to get dressed.

***

"A sauna? You have a sauna and didn't say anything for over a month?" she asks when we reach the old shed I converted into a sauna a few years ago when I had nothing else to do and I was bored out of my mind.

It's a small shed out in the middle of the trees a few yards from the cabin. Its chimney is steaming with smoke from the fire I lit an hour ago to heat it to the temperature we need.

"Did you really want to get naked with me a month ago?" I raise my eyebrow, challenging her.

She looks at me, opens her mouth twice to say something, but then closes it and turns to the sauna. "You've got a point," she mumbles, then points toward the shed. "Are we going in, or are we freezing here to death?" she asks louder.

I open the door for her to enter the small entryway that can barely fit the both of us. I have to bend my neck to avoid bumping the low ceiling.

"We can undress here and leave our clothes, so they don't get wet," I suggest, pointing at the small cabinet next to the door leading to the sauna.

Wendy Ashford—The grump and the chef

She nods as she starts to undress, my erection already awakening in my pants. When we sit down on the bench inside the sauna, rivulets of humidity are already dripping down the small window in the room. The inside of this place is simple—I didn't have much to work with—but the result isn't bad. It's all wood, including the two benches against the longer sides of the shed, and on the opposite wall from the door stands a wood-burning stove with a pot of melted snow that's already boiling.

I put firewood into the stove and watch Olivia close her eyes and inhale deeply, seated opposite me. She's a vision with her pale skin starting to glisten with perspiration. She opens one eye and smiles at me.

"Are you enjoying the view?" she asks, opening both eyes and smiling seductively.

I like when she's flirty with me. "Yes."

She puts a foot on the bench next to my thigh, then the other on the opposite side of my body, spreading her legs wide. Nothing is hidden about her beautiful body. My cock stands to attention, and she licks her lips, watching it twitch between my legs.

"Is that better?" she meows seductively.

She's not a tease, but she has a way of flirting that's even more erotic. "Definitely."

"Do you want to do something about it?" she asks, tilting her head and challenging me.

I drop to my knees in front of her. The space is so tight my cock rests against her pussy, just the right height to fuck her easily. I grab both her ankles in each of my hands and push them high over her head. She gasps and bites her lips, blushing a bit at the obscene pose that gives me access to both her holes.

I rub my cock over her clit, and she closes her eyes, panting.

"Look at me." My voice comes out low and raspy. "I want you to look at me while I sink deep into that tight pussy of yours."

She looks straight into my eyes while I align my cock to her opening and sink slowly into her. She's so wet I glide right in. In this position, I can spread her legs wider and deepen my push until I fill her up. She whimpers in pleasure when my tip touches that sweet spot that gives her shivers.

I draw back until I pull almost out and then push my hips forward, thrusting with force into her. She moans, grabbing my arms to counter my thrust, her tits bouncing in front of me. I go slow, enjoying her groans every time I slam into her.

"Please, Noah, fuck me. Fuck me already," she pleads.

"As you wish," I grin down at her and increase my pace.

I fuck her a bit rough, the way she likes it. My hips slapping against her ass is the only sound you can hear,

Wendy Ashford—The grump and the chef

mixed with our moaning and groaning. She comes with a guttural cry, and I come with her.

I lower her legs and drag her toward my chest. She wraps her arms tightly around my neck and hugs me, resting her forehead on the hollow of my neck.

"I love your sauna," she pants.

I burst out laughing. "I knew I'd use it sooner or later."

"We can use it any time you want." She laughs too.

We stay for a while, her sitting on my lap on the bench, cuddling together without saying a word. It's relaxing until Olivia stands up abruptly.

"You know what we should do now?" she asks enthusiastically, and I start to sweat, not because of the sauna but because her ideas are sometimes weird and dangerous.

"I'm afraid to ask," I admit.

"We should do like the Northern Europeans and go out naked in the snow."

"Are you crazy? We'll catch a cold. We're not used to it." I grab her wrist as she tries to run outside naked.

She rolls her eyes and pulls free of my grip. "Just for a few minutes. We're not going to die. And by the way, it's a myth that you can get a cold if you're not properly covered," she says as she runs out of the sauna, screaming when she hits the snow. I watch her run knee-deep in it, stumble, and fall face-first in the white powder. She lets out a scream and then laughs her head off.

"You gotta try it! It's amazing!"

"Not a chance! I love my lungs right where they are. I'd rather not cough them out of my body," I answer, putting my clothes on before this place cools down.

The door is still open. When I finally manage to get something on, struggling to drag the fabric over my damp skin, I bring her clothes out.

"Put on something before you die of pneumonia." I cover her with her jacket.

"God, you're obsessed with pneumonia. It's not like everyone dies of it," she answers, putting on her jacket and boots.

We reach the cabin with her naked and walking in front of me.

"You're doing everything in your power to prove me right," I mumble, and she turns around to roll her eyes at me.

Hours later, she's shivering under the blanket in my room with a fever and a cold.

"You were right. I'm dying of pneumonia," she whines and sneezes for the umpteenth time.

I chuckle and put the tray with some hot tea and soup on the nightstand. I sit on the bed next to her as she sits up straight. "No, you're not. You have just a cold. Here, eat something."

"What is it?" She tries to sniff, but her nose is clogged.

"Just chicken soup, nothing fancy."

Wendy Ashford—The grump and the chef

She looks at me, horrified. "Did you kill Rooster to feed me?"

"No, I had some chicken in the freezer!" Does she really think I'd kill the rooster to make soup? I'm not a monster.

"I don't trust you." She puts the soup back on the tray.

I go downstairs, grab the confused rooster, and return, putting it on my bed. She nods like I just showed her proof of my integrity, then she cups the little guy's head between her hands like she's covering his ears. "Now bring him downstairs. He can probably smell his relatives in here!" She whisper-shouts it, and I look at her, dumbfounded.

"Are you serious?" I whisper-shout back. Why am I not speaking like a grown-ass adult?

She nods furiously, and before she freaks out, I grab the rooster and, as I'm walking down the stairs, I realize I'm taking a freaking rooster up and down just because she asked me, just because I want her to be happy. I'm pretty sure this means I'm in deep trouble.

# Chapter 15

Noah and I are both sitting on the couch reading books when his phone rings. He frowns, looks at it like it's going to explode, then at me in panic as if he doesn't know what to do.

"Aren't you going to answer that?" I ask when I see he doesn't move.

"Why?" He stares at me like I just suggested he should parade around Main Street naked.

"Because someone is calling you?" I'm a bit confused about what his problem is.

"Nobody calls me. Ever," he replies, like it's the most obvious answer to my confusion.

"Especially if you don't answer your phone. They probably give up." I can't hide a smile.

The phone stops ringing as Noah gives me the side eye. Not a minute later, the phone starts ringing again. I huff, stand up, and grab the evil device from the cabinet.



Wendy Ashford—The grump and the chef

"This is Noah's cabin. How may I help you?" I answer at Noah's horrified gaze. He looks almost disgusted.

"Why does it sound like you have a potato up your nose?" Ava asks me from the other side of the line.

"I got a cold yesterday," I answer, perplexed.

Noah raises his eyebrow inquisitively. *"Ava,"* I mouth to him, and he makes a face as if to say, *"See? Nobody calls me!"* I roll my eyes and sit back on my spot on the couch next to him.

"Did you run around naked in the snow?" she teases, and I blush. She has no idea that's exactly what I did, right after Noah fucked me silly in the sauna.

"Sort of. Never mind. Why are you calling? Is everything okay? Is my mom giving you a hard time?" Bombarding her with questions is the best way to avoid an embarrassing explanation.

"Your mom is calling me daily, but that's not why I reached out," she explains, and I feel bad. My mom can be really stressful sometimes. It's a wonder she hasn't sent anyone to rescue me yet.

"I'm sorry about that. I'll try to call her more often and tell her to cut you some slack." Not that I'm expecting her to listen to me. She's stubborn when she gets obsessed with something.

"Don't worry about it. I'm figuring out how to handle her."

"Really?" I'm stunned. I'm her daughter, and I have yet to learn how to survive in her presence without being overwhelmed by her anxiety.

I hear her chuckle. "I miss you."

"I miss you too. But you're not calling to say that, right? What happened?" I'm starting to get a bit worried.

Next to me, Noah is not even pretending anymore to read his book. He's watching me, and I swear there's concern on his face. It's strange, our relationship. We're having sex and sharing intimate moments living together, but we're not a couple. At least, I don't think so. We've never talked about the future, about what will happen when the snow melts, and I'm not forced to be here anymore. On some level, we skipped dating and went straight to living together.

"A friend of mine told me there's going to be an opening for a senior editor position soon at his publishing company. He asked if I knew someone, and I told him you're looking. I sent him your resume, and he asked if you'd agree to an interview."

"Oh," is all I can say. Because the truth is, I came here to take a break, regroup and think about my future, but since I've been stuck in this cabin, I haven't thought once about going back to New York and finding another job.

I've been using being stuck here as an excuse for not doing any research online, but the reality is, I don't

Wendy Ashford—The grump and the chef

have any idea of what to look for. My dream growing up was to open my own restaurant, and when I found my job at the publishing company, I convinced myself it was just a way to make money to pursue my dream. But then routine settled in, and reality knocked at my door. I'll never have enough money to open a restaurant in New York, and I realize I have to find another dream. Is working at a publishing company my ultimate goal? I don't know. I never hated my job, but I never loved it either. It was just okay; I never felt the urge to dedicate my life to it.

When I stepped into this cabin, it was like I left reality back in New York. I've been living in this bubble where everything is simple, I have no major concerns, and problems are easy to solve. But this is not *my* reality. It's Noah's, and I don't belong here. I wouldn't survive one week if he weren't here.

"Don't be so overly enthusiastic about the news." She chuckles, and I realize I went silent after my non-reply.

"Sorry, I don't know what to say. It's terrific news you found me a job, but I'm stuck here until spring, and I don't know if they'll wait for me." It occurs to me that the idea of not making it to the interview is more exciting than the idea of doing it. I have the feeling this is a massive red flag waving in front of my eyes, but I dismiss it as soon as it enters my mind.

I feel Noah tensing next to me, and when I look at him, his face is a mask of hard, cold feelings. He wasn't even this grim when we first met.

She scoffs. "Find a way to come back. Walk down the mountain if you have to, but I can't hold that position for months. It'll be gone as soon they post it on their website."

She seems almost offended that I don't consider risking my life for this job. I mean, it *is* a huge opportunity. It's not often something like this gets served to you on a silver platter, but it's not enough of a reason to risk my life, or Noah's, to go back to town and hop on a bus. I can't ask something like that to him, no matter how massive this opportunity is.

"I'll let you know if I figure something out," I tell her, not shutting her proposal down completely. I don't want to seem ungrateful after she went out of her way to put my name out there.

"Good. Because I miss you, and even if you are having the best sex of your life with your mountain man, I want you here. You left me alone for Thanksgiving. I don't want to be alone again for Christmas."

I hear the sadness in her voice. She's my best friend, and I miss her too. Guilt squeezes my chest. God, I never once felt remorse about not being with her during the holidays. This is not how a good best friend should be acting. "It's literally in five days. I don't think I can make it back to New York by Christmas," I blurt out as an excuse.

174

She chuckles. "I'm surprised you didn't deny the best sex of your life part."

"Ava!" I feel my face burn and glance at Noah, but I don't see his usual amused smirk when my friend and I talk about sex. He seems angry, with his nose buried in his book and a white-knuckled grip on those pages. The muscles in his jaw tick like he's grinding his teeth. I force myself to focus on my conversation with my best friend and not on the angry guy next to me.

She chuckles again. "Find a way to come back, okay? I'll try to buy you some time, but I can't promise that job will still be there in the spring."

"Thank you," I murmur before hanging up.

I put the phone on the couch when Noah stands up abruptly. At my feet, Jack perks up his ears.

"Where are you going?" I frown at his sudden need to leave the room.

"To find a way to bring you back," he says in a deadly tone.

It takes me a few seconds to understand the meanings of his words. "What? Why?"

He stops next to the couch and finally looks me in the eyes. There is anger, maybe a little bit of disappointment, and a glimpse of sadness in his. The mood change is so sudden my head spins.

"You have to go back to New York, right?" His words are clipped, as though the conversation causes him physical pain. I know we haven't talked much lately about the development of our relationship, but he seems to be overreacting about this phone call.

"I can't go back! There's literally six feet of snow at the front door!" I protest.

"But you have that job interview, right?" he spits out angrily.

I don't understand why he's angry with me. It's not my fault Ava called me about that. I told her I can't go back until spring. He's acting like I did something wrong, and anger boils in my veins.

"So what? That doesn't change the fact that I can't go back. Or did you magically fix that snowmobile overnight? Because I don't see how the situation is any different from this morning."

He's becoming even angrier. What is his problem?

"But if you could, you'd jump on it without looking back. You'd find a perfect new job in your old shiny city and forget about the six feet of snow at the front door. Am I right?" He's almost trembling, fighting his feelings.

Is he angry because I have to go back? He's the one who didn't want me here in the first place. I mean, the sex is great, but he lives in a freaking cabin and avoids human contact. Now he's making a scene because, at some point, I have to go back. Is he serious?

"What should I do? Mooch off of you up here for the rest of my life?" I ask in disbelief. "I don't have unlimited amounts of money flowing into my bank account. I need a job to survive."

Wendy Ashford—The grump and the chef

"Yeah, sure, do whatever you want," he murmurs, giving me his back and walking toward the back door to the garage.

"What do you want from me, Noah? What?" I shout angrily. I don't understand why he's so furious with me about a job offer I didn't ask for and a situation I can't change.

He turns around and nails me to the couch with a livid look. But there's something else mixed with it. Hurt. Noah is hurt by my conversation with Ava, and I don't know what to do with this information, and it throws me off balance.

"Nothing. I want nothing from you!" he shouts back before slamming the door behind him, rattling the doggy door in the process.

Jack whines next to me. He looks up, and I swear there is concern in his eyes. "What the hell just happened?" I ask him. He doesn't have an answer, and neither do I.

# Chapter 16

It's been six hours since I fought with Olivia. Six hours spent fixing this damn snowmobile, fuming like never before. I haven't been this angry since my ex left me, and even then, I wasn't so much angry as humiliated and heartbroken. I didn't feel the blood boiling in my veins in an irrational reaction to some news I should have expected.

The truth is, I know sooner or later she'll be gone. Under normal circumstances, she'd never willingly choose to live up here buried in the snow for months without being able to leave if things got suffocating. What did I expect? That stellar sex would change something?

It was unfair to bark at her, but I couldn't stop myself. It's like I opened a dam and poured out all my fear and anger on her without explaining why.

Jack strolls into the garage, wagging his tail. He stops a few feet from me as though to gauge if I'm still mad or not.

Wendy Ashford—The grump and the chef

"I'm not a monster, okay?" I reach out to scratch his snout. His tail wags against the side of the snowmobile. "But I was an ass, wasn't I?" I ask when he rests his head on my legs. "I didn't mean to scare you."

He whines like he wants to confirm that I acted like an asshole and freaked them both out. I think this is the first time he's seen me so distressed, and I don't know what to do.

I should go inside and apologize to her, but what would I say? That I was an asshole because somehow I hoped she'd choose to stay? I can't even admit to myself that I probably care about her more than I thought, and I don't know how to explain it to her without sounding like a weirdo.

What if she wants to try having a relationship and asks me to leave this place for her? I've never lived an adult life outside this cabin. I don't have a college degree, let alone any specific job skills. I work where I'm needed—cutting trees or moving pallets in a warehouse, but nothing that requires a particular skill. I'm handy, but that isn't enough to find a job.

And what if she wants to move to New York? I've never been outside this state. Hell, I've never been outside this county. How could I follow her to a big, chaotic city? What would I even do there?

I stare at the snowmobile and think about how terrifying it is to consider giving up this life, not knowing if she wants a future with me. I don't know what's

worse—the idea of moving out of this cabin or facing her rejection.

I close my eyes, rub a hand over my face, and sigh deeply. "God, I'm such an idiot," I mumble as I scratch Jack's ears.

The snowmobile in front of me is fixed. At least, I think it is. Every piece is back in place. The only way to be sure is to try and start it, but I can't bring myself to do it. If it really works, I have no excuse to keep her here, and I can't muster the courage to let her go. Not yet. I'll do it. I'm not trying to be a creepy psycho who locks a woman in my basement, but I need to come to terms with her being gone for good. I can wait a few hours to see if I actually fixed this thing.

I stand up, Jack complaining at having to get up, too, and wash my hands before going back inside. I find Olivia at the stove, cooking something for dinner. When she looks up, she smiles, but it never reaches her eyes. She's pissed and maybe a little sad, but she's too polite to insult me. She'd have every right to, but she's not like that. Olivia's cheerful, outgoing, not vindictive. She'd never hurt me on purpose.

"Sit," she orders, pointing to the stool near the counter.

I do as she says and sit down, waiting for her. She grabs a towel, wets a corner of it, and then grabs my face between two fingers and starts to rub. "You have streaks of grease all over your face."

Wendy Ashford—The grump and the chef

I smile. "I probably rubbed my face while I was fixing the snowmobile." I almost tell her that I think it's working, but the words get stuck in my throat.

She finishes cleaning my face, goes back to the stove to check dinner, and then serves us two plates. We eat in silence, something I'm not used to anymore. I try a few times to open my mouth and say something, but she stares at her plate, not giving me an opening to apologize.

We started to get close for real so recently, and I've already fucked it up. I deserve to live and die alone on this mountain.

We clean the kitchen side by side, synchronized like an old couple that's been doing this for years. I never noticed it until tonight, and I feel a sense of dread invading my chest. I should have kept my distance and protected my heart like I'd planned to all these years. Instead, here I am pining for a woman who's not mine and never will be. I wish I could bring her back to town right now, rip off the band-aid, and deal with the hurt and bleeding and emotional mess that comes with it.

But I don't. I grab the deck of cards instead and sit on the floor in front of the fireplace, dealing out her hand of cards and then mine. She seems to hesitate for a second but then decides to give me a chance.

I lose the first hand on purpose, giving her the chance to come up with a dare to punish me. She doesn't even look at me in the eyes when she drops the bomb. "I dare you to go up to your room and sleep alone tonight."

I sit frozen, baffled at her clear intentions. Since we've started having sex, I just assumed we would sleep in the same bed for the rest of her stay here, but obviously, she has other plans for tonight. Only now do I notice the blanket and pillow on the corner of the couch.

I put down my cards, stand up, and move toward the stairs. I stop and open my mouth to say something, but she never looks at me, so I shut it and go upstairs. Knowing I deserve this punishment doesn't make it any less painful. With every step, I feel the distance grow between us. What we had was something new and fragile, and I barged in, stomping on all the tender words and feelings we shared together, ruining any chance of fixing the mess I've made.

# Chapter 17

I stared at the ceiling all night. I tried to close my eyes, but every time the discussion with Noah took center stage in my thoughts, I found myself sighing out loud and opening my eyes, like I could find an answer written on the wooden beams of the cabin. I thought a lot about it, and I still can't understand why he was upset with me.

I have to go back to New York, right? I need to sort out my life and think about moving on, I can't hide here for the rest of my existence. Even if the temptation is almost overwhelming, I have a life there I can't ignore. Was it perfect—what I left behind before I ended up here? No, but it was still something I built and fought to be happy for.

My mom, dad, and Ava are in New York. They're the pillars of my entire existence. I can't ignore them, even if it is easier to stay in these mountains and pretend I'm not homeless and jobless. At some point, I'd have to contribute to the expenses, and my bank account isn't a fat source of money. It's pretty skinny, to be honest. I don't come from a rich family, and living in Manhattan is not exactly cheap. I'm not his girlfriend, either, and I shouldn't even be thinking those thoughts at this point.

The creak of the stairs tells me that Noah's coming down. I didn't want to talk to him yesterday; I was still too angry, but I can't ignore him forever, especially because he seems way too rational and levelheaded to freak out like he did. There must be a reason he reacted so strongly, even if I don't understand it.

"Hey." His voice is gruff, and considering the dark circles under his eyes, I don't think he slept a lot, either.

"Hey," I answer, sitting up and making room for him.

I don't know how to break the ice after yesterday, but he relieves me of my misery and says, "Listen, I'm sorry about how I treated you." He stares at his hands for a long moment before lifting his gaze to mine. There is genuine concern on his face. "I overreacted to the news. I have no right to tell you what to do or not to do."

"I have to go back at some point. I can't hide here and pretend my problems don't exist," I explain.

He nods and lowers his gaze again to the hands on his lap. "I know. I freaked out. As you probably picked up living with me, I don't deal well with big changes in my life. I was just getting used to having you here.

Wendy Ashford—The grump and the chef

I thought I had a few more months before I had to go back to town, and I freaked out when I realized I'll have to do it way sooner."

I feel the disappointment filling my chest. I thought, *hoped*, his reaction was because he cares about me in a way he doesn't want to admit. I'm not someone who carelessly jumps in bed with some attractive guy. I thought that maybe, considering we're stuck together, we could have some fun, but I realized as soon as we had sex, it was not just physical attraction I feel for him. I trust him enough to get completely naked in front of him without feeling embarrassed about my weight.

I spent every single day of my life feeling self-conscious about my appearance, but the way Noah looks at me—like I'm the most beautiful woman on the planet—is enough to make my doubt disappear. He makes me feel confident and powerful, and that's not something you ignore in a relationship. But we don't have a relationship. We're just having fun. The sex is spectacular, but that's it. At least for him, apparently. As for me, I don't know what I want. At least, not rationally. My heart is another story entirely.

I swallow my pride and put a smile on my face. "The plan hasn't changed. I still have to stay here until spring. Unless you can melt the snow, which would be freaky, but I'd be able to go to town sooner."

He smiles at my joke, but he doesn't seem amused. I feel the rift between us almost physically. It's strange how much I've grown attached to this guy without even realizing it.

"I fixed the snowmobile. I just need to try and start it, but I'm pretty sure there won't be a problem," he says, and my chest hurts like a bomb just detonated in it.

I should be happy, right? This is exactly what I wanted. So, why do I feel like my heart dropped into my stomach and has no intention of climbing back up? Like I'm drowning.

I force a smile. "You finally found a way to get rid of me!" I chirp with too much enthusiasm to sound natural.

He looks at me for a long moment, almost like he wants to say something, but then thinks twice about it. It's just a glimpse, but it's there. A raw sadness that disappears as fast as it crosses his face. My heart makes a strange flip in my chest.

"You can go back to do that job interview. And while you're at it, rub in your ex's face the fact that he was an idiot to let you go," he finally says.

A half-laugh leaves my lips before I can even try to stop it. I haven't thought about Greg for one second lately. He's so far from my mind, he could be part of another life entirely. God, and to think I wanted to marry him. What a massive mistake that would've been.

"Yeah. *If* I get the job. It's not as easy as it sounds. If they ask for references from my previous job, I doubt he'll support me." And I don't know if I want that job, but I don't tell him that. I'm not sure how I feel about it, either. This is the safe choice, the most reasonable one. So, why does it seem so wrong and suffocating?

"I'm sure you'll nail that interview. And your ex will cooperate if he doesn't want to explain your relationship to HR." He's trying to be supportive, but there's no conviction in his voice. "Anyway, if you want to take a shower, I'll check and see if the snowmobile starts, and then I can make us some breakfast," he suggests, and all I can do to keep from crumbling under the weight of emotion is nod and watch his back as he walks to the back door and disappears behind it.

A couple of minutes later, when I hear the grumble of the snowmobile in the garage, my heart splits in two and I sob, the shower washing the tears from my face. It takes me forty minutes to get myself together and walk out of the bathroom without looking like I just had a complete meltdown.

Noah is at the kitchen counter sipping his coffee. When he sees me, he tries to smile and fails. God, why is it so hard to look at him and not want to cry again? Not even when Greg dumped me did I feel this—like the earth is shifting under my feet, ready to crack open and swallow me whole.

"It's fixed. As soon as this storm passes, I can bring you back to town," he states.

I just nod because I don't trust the words coming out of my mouth. I get closer to him, and all I can do right now is put my arms around his neck and hug him. I'll miss him. I'll miss our banters and our stupid dares. I'll miss reading next to him and cooking for him. I'll miss the kisses and the sex. And I'll miss him too.

He puts his arms around my body and hugs me fiercely. I almost can't breathe, but I don't care. I kiss his neck, just below his ear, and he shivers, hugging me even more tightly. He grabs my chin with a couple of fingers and tips my head up. He looks at me for a long moment before kissing me.

He does it slowly, savoring every stroke of my tongue. He does it sweetly, like he doesn't want to shatter the precarious emotions raging in our chests. There's a connection between us we're both afraid to lose. I can feel it in my bones. Something has shifted, and we can't go back.

He grips my butt with one hand as he slides the other into my hair, fisting it in a possessive grip. A moan escapes my lips as he backs me up against the armrest of the couch and tips me over, then follows me until we're both sprawled on top of it. His thick thighs are nestled between mine, and I press my hips against his. His erection is hard against my clit and even with clothes between us, it sends a shiver of pleasure down my spine. I arch against his chest, pressing my aching nipples against his perfect pecs.

We stay on the couch for a long time, kissing, taking our time getting undressed, and making love with a dedication and sweetness I didn't even imagine was possible. There isn't the usual rush, chasing pleasure and giving in quickly to our attraction for each other. The chemistry has changed and evolved into a deeper connection I'm not sure even the distance can lessen. I find myself fighting back tears because I know this experience has forever changed my life. This cabin, these days trapped under feet of snow, changed not only my present and my future but also a part of me I know I'll never have back. Do I regret it? Not even a little bit.

# Chapter 18

I open my eyes. I'm wrapped in Noah's arms, still on the couch where we ended up yesterday and where we made love three times last night. I look at the back of the couch, and sure enough, Rooster is watching us.

"You know you're a creepy little dude, don't you?" I murmur, my voice raspy.

I can feel Noah's chest shake with a chuckle. "This is the first time I've woken up with him staring at me. He really is creepy."

I kiss his chest and wrap a leg over his. I turn my head, and my smile disappears as my heart drops into my stomach. It's sunny. I never thought seeing a slice of sunshine out the window would feel so awful.

Snowstorms usually last for days here, sometimes even a week. I'm dreading the moment I have to get up and start packing my things—which isn't even that much. It will take me half-hour, max, to pack my suitcase, and that's if I fold all my clothes carefully.

190

"It's sunny." Noah's raspy voice sounds like a bucket of cold water dumped on my head. He noticed too. Of course, he noticed. It's not like you can miss the bright sun streaming through the window. It's like God is illuminating the path back to my normal life. Well, I needed this miracle two months ago, not now!

Noah tightens the grip around my body as though sensing the tumultuous rampage of feelings in my chest. I need to get a grip, or I won't be able to step a foot outside this place.

"I should get up and pack," I say after a long silence.

He doesn't answer for a while, then he kisses the top of my forehead and sits up. His face is unreadable, and my anxiety escalates a bit more. I'm usually good at reading people and gauging their feelings, but Noah is a book in a foreign language I don't understand.

"Yeah, you should," he mumbles without looking me in the eyes.

I take my time putting everything inside my suitcase, but I have so few things to pack it only takes fifteen minutes. Half the time I estimated, but it makes sense. I wasn't planning to stay this long when I flew from New York. In the meantime, Noah is cooking breakfast silently, and the air between us feels heavy. Is it me, or is it harder to breathe today?

I sit at the counter next to him and eat without saying a word. From time to time, he glances at me like he wants to say something, but he never says a word.

Noah is not one for big speeches, but today he's particularly quiet. I'm dying to know what's on his mind. Does he feel this weight on his chest too?

I help him clean the dishes, and when I put on my jacket, Jack starts wagging his tail and whining like he knows I'm not coming back. I'll miss him too. God, I'll even miss Rooster staring at me every morning.

I crouch down and hug Jack. "You're a very good boy. It was a pleasure to share the couch with you," I whisper, kissing his head and standing up.

He whines and barks while following us into the garage. Noah opens the door to the front yard and a knot forms in my throat. He's already strapped my suitcase onto the back of the snowmobile. He pushes it into the yard and starts it, then motions for me to get on. I straddle the seat while he closes the garage door, and Jack protests. I think he wants to follow us, or maybe he just senses my sadness and discomfort.

Noah sits in front of me. I wrap my arms around his waist and tighten my grip while he takes off along what I assume is the road that leads to town. It's an eerie feeling. Everything is white and sparkling and sunny. It feels like stepping into a fairytale, but the weight clogging my chest is almost unbearable. Every foot down the road and farther from the cabin is another tear in my heart.

It takes us half an hour to reach the town. Noah goes slowly, and I don't know if it's because he doesn't trust

Wendy Ashford—The grump and the chef

the packed snow, is worried I'll get scared, or some other reason entirely. Under normal circumstances, it would've probably taken half the time to get here on a snowmobile cutting between the trees.

When we reach Pinecreek, he parks on the side of the road, grabs my suitcase, and guides me to the front of the only grocery store in town. I notice a few people looking out of the windows of the houses along Main Street, no doubt wondering what Noah is doing here with a woman at his side. It's probably not something they're used to, considering the hermit he is.

"The only place that sells bus tickets is the grocery store. We don't have a real bus station." He points to the wooden bench under the bus shelter on the other side of the street. His face is a grim mask I can barely look at.

I nod, not trusting my voice. I swallow a couple of times before attempting to speak. "Thank you for everything." My voice cracks, and I want to wrap my arms around him, but he keeps a distance between us that feels like a mile.

He puts his hands in his jeans pockets. "I'll bring back the rental car when the snow melts, so you don't have to come back and do it yourself. I think if you call them and explain the situation, they'll understand." His voice is as rough as mine. Maybe he's just as affected by this separation as me, but he sure doesn't show it. What did I expect? Tears and pleas to not go?

"Thank you. I really appreciate that," I say without looking him in the eyes.

I feel the lump in my throat growing bigger with every second that passes. There is a long, awkward silence before he speaks again. "Have a safe trip home," he whispers, bending down and kissing my cheek.

I nod with a sad smile on my face, my eyes stinging with tears. I watch him turn around and walk to the snowmobile. The first sob shakes my chest at the same moment Noah starts it and turns back toward his cabin.

I stand there until I can't see him or hear the rumble of the motor going up the mountain, feeling like a fool for letting my heart grow so attached to him. I shiver at the cold, finally finding the strength to go inside the grocery store to buy a bus ticket to the airport.

"Are you okay?" A worried man in his sixties looks at me from behind the counter.

I nod and try to smile even as tears keep streaming down my cheeks. I'm sure I look like a mess. "Yes. I need a ticket for the Seattle-Tacoma airport," I tell him between hiccups.

He stares at me for a long moment, maybe to discern if I really am okay. I force a smile, and I don't know if he buys it—I'm having a hard time convincing myself I'm okay, never mind someone else.

"You'll have to change busses a couple of times to get there," he explains, as though wanting to be sure I know what I'm getting myself into. I didn't expect

194

there to be a shuttle from here straight to the airport. This isn't exactly a tourist spot.

I take a deep breath and try to calm down before he decides I'm not safe traveling alone. "I understand. It's fine." My voice comes out more confident this time.

He takes a deep breath and moves to a computer next to the cash register. He tampers with it for a good five minutes, takes my payment, then gives me a printed ticket.

"The next bus will be here in an hour and a half. Do you want to wait in here? It's cold outside." His voice is softer now, his expression a mixture of pity and kindness that makes my heart clench in my chest. Do I look as desperate as I feel?

"It's okay. I'll wait out there. I don't want to miss it." I hope my explanation is enough to appease his worries.

He nods, and I feel his eyes on my back as I walk outside. I cross the street and sit down on the bench at the bus stop, seeing him watch me through the window. His worried gaze never leaves me until I step on the bus. When I turn around before the doors close, he waves with a sad smile.

*** 

It takes me eight hours to reach my destination, and it's way past midnight when I step foot inside the airport. On the bus ride, I was able to book a last-minute flight to JFK, leaving tomorrow morning, and now I have to sit and wait for my gate information and board-ing time.

The ride here was a whirlwind of emotions I couldn't control. I didn't think two months with a man would make me miss him so much, not even twen-ty-four hours after I'd left.

I grab my phone, and though it's way too early in New York, I call Ava. She answers on the third ring. "If you're calling from your phone, you must've found a way to come down from that mountain," she whispers groggily from the other side of the line.

"Yes," my answer is cut short by a hiccup.

"Are you crying?" she asks, more awake now. Wor-ry permeates her voice.

"Yes," is the only thing I can say without choking.

I hear a deep breath, the rustling of covers, and the click of her nightstand lamp. "Do you want to talk about it?" Her tone softens.

"What do you want me to say?" I whisper.

"Are you in love with him?"

Hearing her say it out loud is like a stab in my chest, eliciting a sob. "I think so," I confess, and my heart aches. Not even when Greg dumped me I felt this des-perate to go back to when everything was okay be-tween us. Why didn't I stop him from fixing that damn thing? But as soon as this thought crosses my mind, I frown. And then what? It wasn't like if I'd stayed until spring, things would be different. My heart sinks a bit more at the thought.

Wendy Ashford—The grump and the chef

There is a long moment of silence.

"Does he know?"

"No. God no. I didn't tell him."

"Why?"

"He doesn't want me." Pain rips through my chest as I tell her that.

"Oh. Did he tell you that?"

"No, but it's not like he tried to stop me from leaving."

There's a long silence on the other end. "Do you want me to stay on the phone with you while you wait to board?" she asks after a minute or two.

"Yes, please," I whisper, drying my tears.

I sit there, letting my confession to Ava sink into my chest. Because the realization of what I just said out loud to my best friend is something I hadn't figured out until now. Noah and I are on different paths. We were great together in the bubble of his cabin, but outside we could never work. He's okay with being holed up in his cabin, but that's not okay for me. I need to do something with my life, and I need to figure it out for myself.

# Chapter 19

I stare at the ceiling, not sure what to do with myself. Since dropping Olivia off at the bus station three days ago, I've been sleeping on the couch. Or at least, trying to. It's small and uncomfortable, but that's not what keeps me awake at night. It's her scent on the pillow and the memory of her in every single square foot of this place.

As soon as I came back and found her books stacked next to the couch, I was almost tempted to go back into town and give them to her. But for what? To make it even harder to let her go? She has a life in New York, and I'm not part of it.

"Don't look at me like that. She couldn't stay forever," I tell Jack, who's been angry with me since I dropped her off.

He stares at me with a scowl. I didn't know a dog could frown, but it's all he is giving me these days. Rooster came in the first night, discovered I wasn't Ol-

198

ivia, and left after a few minutes. He *is* a creepy little guy, completely obsessed with her.

Jack huffs, turns his head toward the door, and ignores me as he's done over the last few days. Traitor. I was his whole world before she showed up at my door.

I sit up and rub a hand over my face. I drag myself to the bathroom and take the shower I've been avoiding for three days. I'm scared if I step under the water, I'll wash away her scent imprinted in my nostrils, my brain. But I'm starting to smell really bad, and I can't go another day without cleaning up.

I step under the warm water, and my brain conjures the image of her on her knees, wrapping her lips around my cock. I look down, almost expecting to see her—that's how strongly I feel her—but the only thing I see is my erection. I don't even try to think about something disgusting to make it go away because the only thing on my mind is Olivia. Her perfect lips, blond hair, and that luscious body I didn't worship enough while she was here. I fist my cock and bring back the feeling of her mouth around it. It only takes a few powerful strokes to come harder than I ever have on my own.

I lean against the cold tiles and breathe deeply. I was perfectly fine here alone in my cabin. A few quick fucks over the summer, and some porn during the winter were all I needed. But she showed me a different reality. One with a woman in my life to share warm hugs, delicious meals, and pillow talk. A life I gave up years ago and never looked back until now.

I wash off the soap and step out of the shower, dry the mirror with a towel, and stare at my reflection. I look like I just crawled out of the bowels of hell. The dark circles under my eyes are the most obvious, but the general tiredness in my face reveals the sleepless nights. I sigh and grip the sink until my knuckles turn white. I can't be like this for a woman I've only known for two months. Okay, so she was the best lay of my life, but I can't be completely heartbroken like this.

I get dressed, walk out of the bathroom, and stroll to the freezer in the garage. I open it to grab something to cook for breakfast, and the first thing I see is a batch of pastries with a note written on it, clearly in Olivia's handwriting: "Don't touch! For Christmas."

My heart sinks into my stomach. Today is Christmas. I hadn't thought much of it; I've always treated it like any other day. But now I can't stop thinking of the "what ifs." What if Olivia were here today? What if I'd told her to stay until spring? What if I flew to New York to be with her?

I don't have any answers, so I grab the pastries, warm them in the oven, and eat them alone on the couch that smells faintly of her. My heart sinks a bit deeper into my stomach. It's a long, lonely, and empty life I see in my future.

200

# Chapter 20

Seated on Ava's couch, I watch my best friend grabbing a couple of glasses and a bottle of red wine. I had Christmas Eve dinner with my mom, Christmas lunch with my dad, and now Christmas dinner with Ava. Or liquid dinner, as she loves to call it. All the calories we will ingest tonight will be wine-provided.

God only knows how much I need to get drunk tonight. It's been three days since I left Noah and I can barely sleep. Every time I close my eyes, I dream about his ripped body on top of mine. But also his smile and his grumpiness, his laughs, and his silences. Noah is a kaleidoscope of facets that I was lucky enough to experience, and I want to explore more.

"So, let's start with the most important thing: he is good in bed, right?" Ava asks when she sits down next to me.

I almost spit out the wine I'm sipping. One thing I didn't miss about Ava is her blatant nosiness. She can be a sweet friend most of the time, but when she decides your sex life is more exciting than hers—which is like, never until now!—she wants to know every sordid detail.

"*That* is the most important thing?" I arch my eyebrow, questioning her.

She sips from her glass and nods. "If you're going to regret *not* having someone in your life, at least he should be a good lay."

"Geez, you sure know how to cheer me up." I take a generous sip of wine. If this is the tone of our conversation, I'd better get drunk and fast. "He is definitely good in bed," I confirm.

"Define good. I need more details," she smirks behind her glass.

I don't think she needs this much information, but she'll never give up, so I go for it. What have I got to lose? "Almost double-digit orgasms in one night— that kind of good." It's my turn to hide behind the glass, blushing when she stares at me wide-eyed, like I sprouted a couple of heads under my sweater.

Something she always remarked on about my relationship with Greg was that I didn't have any orgasms with him. She'd point out how he was a selfish prick, and I would defend him, saying that maybe I was the one incapable of feeling pleasure. Noah proved me wrong many times. He showed me that a man can wor-

ship a woman's body in so many ways that she can actually experience orgasm-induced soreness.

She grabs my half-empty glass and tops it with more wine. "Honey, if that's true, you need more alcohol."

"I know. I think the only way to get Noah out of my head is drinking so much I'll erase every memory of him." No chance in the world I can survive otherwise.

"So, you're in love, huh?" Her voice softens, and her expression is cautious. It's like she's watching a wild animal and gauging its reaction. I *feel* like a wild animal right now. Like I'm trapped in some sort of cage, and I'm going crazy trying to figure out how to escape. The problem is that the cage is in my head, and I can't run away from that.

I inhale deeply. "Is it even possible after not even two months of knowing a person?"

She takes her time to answer. "Two months of dating in Manhattan, maybe not, but two months stuck in a cabin with a man twenty-four-seven, things move fast."

"I guess that's true," I sigh.

"Think about it. You know his most intimate habits, which you normally don't discover about a significant other until you move in together. Which often breaks up a solid relationship. You skipped all the steps and moved into the most intense and stressful part of a relationship. So, yes. I suppose you can be in love after not even two months," she adds softly.

I stare at my glass, not knowing what to say. I hoped she'd tell me it's only a phase, that it's not possible, and to get over it. The sadness that expands in my chest is almost suffocating.

"Or you could be orgasm-blinded and testosterone-intoxicated. Maybe that's a reason too. I never had double-digit orgasms in my entire life, so I'm playing it by ear." She chuckles, and I half-laugh too.

"God. I didn't know sex could be so intense. He did things to my body I didn't know were possible." I hide my face behind my free hand.

Ava laughs heartily, throwing her head back. "So, he has a good package."

I blush. "It's not just that. He worships my body like he wants to eat me alive. And he did! A lot. I've never had a thing for oral sex, but he ruined me. They should sculpt a giant marble replica of his tongue and put it in a museum."

Ava is bent over on the couch laughing, and I can't stop thinking about the fabulous sex I've had lately. "Did you at least return the favor?" she asks when she calms down.

"I tried my best, but I couldn't fit it all in my mouth," I confess.

Ava bursts into another fit of giggles, but when she calms down, her look becomes serious. "So, what are you doing here in Manhattan?"

I don't know. Honestly, since returning, I've started to wonder what the hell I should do here. All the people I love live here, but is it enough to stay? Returning to the city, I've always considered my home after almost two months away should be exciting, right? I didn't feel enthusiastic seeing the Manhattan skyline in the taxi from the airport.

"I have a job interview in two days, thanks to you. And I still have all my things here."

"That's true, but the interview is for a job you don't love, and your things are in storage. It's the same effort to ship them to the other coast as it would be to an apartment here in Manhattan," she points out, and she's right.

I say nothing for a long moment because I don't have an answer for what she's implying. I know I care about him, but I don't know what *he* thinks about me. "He doesn't do relationships, so I don't see the point in changing my life," I confess.

"Did you ask him if he was interested?" she insists.

I get defensive. "No, but he put me on a snowmobile the first chance he got and drove me to town. I think it's safe to say he doesn't want me there."

"Or maybe he wants to give you a chance to fix what you left here in New York instead of delaying the inevitable. It's true that you can't just disappear from your old life and start another one somewhere else, but it's also true that you can change the course of the one you have. Deal with what you have here, so you don't have strings attached, but then choose what's best for you." She smiles sweetly at me.

She makes it sound so easy, but the thought is so scary I don't even try to contemplate it. A new job as a senior editor? I know exactly what to do. I became comfortable over the years with this career. Thinking about an entirely new career, one I don't even know about yet? A whole other level of stress. I like stability and routine, something I know how to navigate. New York is safe. Pinecreek? It's a pit of uncertainty. I move there and—what—hope Noah changes his mind in the relationship department?

"Or maybe I was the only one falling," I whisper, and with that, Ava has nothing to say.

But on one point, she's right. I need to fix things here in New York. I can't imagine living in my mother's spare room and fishing my stuff out of storage. I need to put my life on track, figure out what I want to do, and make a plan.

***

I walk into the white ultra-modern reception area of C&B Publishing in Midtown fifteen minutes earlier than my interview appointment with the chief editor. He's Ava's friend from college, and he promised her he would personally take care of me.

"I'm here to see Mr. Cortese. My name is Olivia Harris. He is waiting for me," I say to the blond girl with a bright smile behind the reception desk.

Wendy Ashford—The grump and the chef

She checks her computer and then nods. "Mr. Cortese can see you now." She stands and gestures for me to follow her.

I keep up with her long strides along the white corridors, the only splashes of color coming from the occasional plants that dot the walls and corridors. The minimalist style works with the modern vibe they're putting out, but it's a bit cold for my taste.

Maybe I got used to the warmth of the log cabin over the last weeks, and this is a stark contrast I don't particularly like. Or maybe I'm nervous about my interview, and I just need to calm down.

I don't have time to think about my nerves because the receptionist knocks at a white anonymous door and then opens it for me to enter. I step into an office with the same white walls and furniture I encountered walking here, and the only splash of color now is the gray suit Mr. Cortese is wearing.

"You must be Olivia. Ava's told me a lot about you," he says, standing up, walking around the desk, and shaking my hand firmly as the receptionist closes the door behind me.

He has a warm smile and a mop of curly dark hair that falls over his forehead. For some reason, his perfectly shaven jaw makes me uncomfortable. It reminds me of Greg, and my stomach clenches in an unpleasant grip.

"Good things, I hope." I smile, sitting in the chair in front of his desk.

He chuckles as he sits in his white leather armchair. God, what's wrong with the interior designer of this place? "She was very vocal in telling me you are the best senior editor I could hire." He winks at me, and while there is no malevolent intent in his gesture, I'm annoyed by it.

I try to pinpoint what it is about this guy I don't like, but I can't come up with anything. He seems a genuinely good person, all warm smiles and a demeanor that makes you feel comfortable. So why don't I?

And the realization crashes over me like a rough wave at sea—unexpected and making me shiver. I don't want to be here. I don't want to interview for this job. This is not what I see in my future. This is just another safe job I won't love but will feel compelled to do. It's a dead end I'm willingly stepping into.

But I don't have to. This time, I can turn around and change my life. It's scary as hell but also liberating. God, I feel so exhilarated I could pee my pants.

"No, I'm not!" I blurt out.

He's taken aback but smiles. "You're not the best editor?"

"No. I'm a very good chef who edited books for years without loving what I was doing."

I'm sorry about Ava. She tried to help me out, and I'm throwing away the opportunity she offered me, but I can't keep going like this. I don't like my job, it makes me miserable, and I know I can be good doing something else.

Wendy Ashford—The grump and the chef

"So, what is your dream job?" he asks, almost chuckling. He knows I'll never walk out of this place with a contract in my hands, but he seems amused by it, not irritated.

"I love to cook." I frown.

"That's not a job," he points out with a smile.

"I know. I just have to figure out how to make it a job." Every word that leaves my lips seems to carry away a bit of the heaviness oppressing my chest. I can finally breathe.

"You had an epiphany coming into this office, didn't you?" He chuckles.

I choke on a laugh. "Yeah, I think so."

He tilts his head and laughs outright. "What triggered it? Why now? It's the white minimalist bullshit decor, isn't it?"

I can't stop a giggle from coming out of my mouth. "God, it's awful. How can you work in a place so bright? Do you wear sunglasses?"

"I swear, at home, I forced my husband to buy the most colorful furniture possible to compensate for the lack of color in my work life." He smirks, but then rests his hands on his desk and studies me for a long moment.

"How does it feel?" he asks after a long silence where I don't know what to do. Should I thank him and walk away?

"What?"

"Realizing that you can follow your dreams."

"The best kind of terrifying." I smile because it's true.

Wendy Ashford—The grump and the chef

# Chapter 21

Two days after Christmas, I'm on my way to town. I can't stand another hour in that cabin without her. I put her books in a closet and cleaned every surface twice so I couldn't smell her anywhere. I washed the sheets three times with more soap than necessary to be sure her scent was definitely gone, but I can't get her out of my head. She's in my t-shirt she wore after we had sex. She's in the pan she cooked most of our meals in because "it's the perfect pan,"—she said. She's in the green towel hanging in the bathroom that wrapped her perfect body so well I almost threw it away because it reminds me so much of her.

The truth is, I'd have to burn the place down with everything I own inside to forget her. She's in everything I do, every space in the house, every memory in my head, every fucking breath I take.

That's why I don't do relationships—they always leave me. First, my mother when I was just a kid, then my ex at the altar, and now Olivia. I'm always the one who has to pick up the pieces when they decide that Pinecreek is not enough for them.

I park the snowmobile behind the grocery store and look around. What the hell am I doing here? Where do I go? People will start to ask questions, considering I haven't come down once in the winter over the last ten years. What can I tell them? They've seen me here twice in less than a week. Because I know they saw me bring her here. This place is deserted during winter; a snowmobile coming down the mountain in the middle of the week and a stranger waiting for a bus not even locals use will not go unnoticed.

I take a deep breath and decide to play it safe and go to the grocery store. At least I have an excuse to buy something, even if Henry will be suspicious. I take a deep breath and open the door. The bell rings, and Henry looks up from behind the counter where he's reading the newspaper.

He frowns. "Did the girl eat all your winter provisions?"

Thinking he would overlook Olivia or my extra trip to town was too much to hope for. But this is the only place she could buy a bus ticket, so it's no surprise he knows.

"No. I need…" I have no idea what I need, so I grab the first thing I see on the shelf. Cornstarch. A massive jug of cornstarch. I'm no chef, but I think this thing

Wendy Ashford—The grump and the chef

will last me ten years. How many things I cook even use cornstarch? The correct answer is zero. But Henry's looking at me with raised eyebrows over my peculiar choice, so I can't put it down now. I pretend to be cool and stroll to the counter with my cornstarch in hand and my dignity squashed under my shoes.

"You fixed that snowmobile after ten years so you could come and buy cornstarch? Must be some recipe you've got planned up there." He struggles to fight back a smile.

I give him a dirty look and pay my thirty dollars for one gallon of this shit. One gallon. Not even a restaurant uses that much cornstarch.

"I needed to fix it, sooner or later," I mumble, not sure what to do now that I'm done at the grocery store. I have to go back to the cabin, don't I?

"Yes. It took you ten years. Or maybe you had a new motive to do it. A blond one. One that cried for an hour and a half sitting on that bench over there, looking for someone to come back." He points a finger toward the window and the bench.

My heart squeezes in my chest. "She cried the whole time?"

He nods. "And I doubt she stopped when she got on the bus."

There's a hint of scolding in his tone that makes me uncomfortable. How did I know she was crying? Maybe I should have stayed and waited with her for the bus. But why? To see her cry the entire time, or to not be able to let her go when the bus came? I hate that she was crying. Why? She wanted to go home for that interview. She wanted nothing to do with this place. She said it: she had to go home to sort her life out. She couldn't hide up here forever. I'm not part of the shit she has to take care of. I'm just a good lay, an adventure she can brag about to her friends when she goes home. But she doesn't seem like the type who brags about stuff like that. Does she?

"Can I ask what happened? Where did she come from? And why do you have that sad face? You never come to town until spring, yet here you are, buying cornstarch like you own a restaurant, not even a week after you show up with a mysterious girl." He lays the truth out in front of me, and I have no hope of hiding. He's known me since I was a kid. There's very little he doesn't know about me.

"She came here the day before the first snow. She meant to stay here in town but ended up in the hunting hut half a mile from my cabin."

"Jesus. That place doesn't even have running water," he breathes out in disbelief.

"I found her the next day. She was scared, and she clearly couldn't take care of herself out in the wild until spring. She's from New York," I explain, and he frowns and nods, understanding my meaning. "So, I offered to take her in until spring. But at some point,

Wendy Ashford—The grump and the chef

she had to go back, so I fixed the snowmobile to bring her here."

"You've been living with her for almost two months?" He seems quite impressed.

"Not that I had a choice," I grumble.

"But now you can't stay away from her," he points out with a knowing smile like he has everything figured out.

"It's not like that."

"Well, it sure seems like it." He beams.

"What do you mean?"

"I think you found a woman who's worth coming down the mountain for."

I say nothing. His remark hits way too close to home. Isn't that why I have a gallon of cornstarch in my hands? She messed with my head and maybe a little bit with my heart, and now I can't pretend that I never met her. Because she's not some meaningless summer hookup; she's someone I could think of having a future with. I don't believe in "The One," not after being dumped at the altar by someone I thought was just that, but I'm starting to believe in "growing old with" because it's something I've been thinking about a lot lately. And she's in my every thought about the future.

"And maybe that house behind the church won't stay empty much longer. Tom is still trying to sell it. If you want, I can tell him you're interested," he adds when he sees me hesitate.



The grump and the chef—Wendy Ashford

"Maybe you didn't notice she went back to New York?" I ask, but my argument is weak.

"So, what are you doing here?" His tone softens, and the warmth in his eyes makes my heart ache. He's always hoped I'd find a girl and settle down. He was the one coming to the bars when my ex first dumped me, looking for my drunk ass to drag home. More of a father to me than my own.

"What am I supposed to do? Go to New York?" I can hear the panic in my voice.

He raises an eyebrow as if to challenge me to contradict him.

"And do what?" I ask the most terrifying question that's been keeping me up at night lately.

"Find a job or bring her back. You can't stay here, buying gallons of cornstarch and moping around."

I look at my shoes. He's right. Like it or not, she changed my life and showed me something I tried to avoid for ten years. A settled life I craved when I was twenty, but I gave up on it when my heart got broken. Olivia woke me up to the fact that I can try to hide and pretend everything is fine, but it's not. Not by a long shot.

"Listen, you got hurt last time, but not every woman is like your ex. At least speak to her; try to figure out if there's something you can save about the relationship. It's not like it can get any worse—she's already left you."

Wendy Ashford—The grump and the chef

I give him the stink eye, but he's got a point. She *has* already left me. Crying. Maybe there is some hope.

***

"Are you nervous?" The kind voice of the woman seated next to me startles me. I turn to see her sweet eyes smiling at me. She's probably in her late sixties and looking a bit concerned about my stiffness.

"A bit," I say through my teeth, tightening the grip on my knees.

She chuckles and pats my hand. "Is it your first flight?" she asks after a beat.

"Yep." I think I'm not even breathing. How do people get into this trap daily and survive it? Seriously. How can a thing this big stay up in the air without falling and crashing? Damn! I shouldn't think about crashing before takeoff.

"She's a lucky lady," she says knowingly.

I hope to survive the flight to tell her that.

# Chapter 22

"Are you sure you don't want to stay for a few days? I can make space in the guest room for you," Ava asks as we stand outside her apartment. She's hugging me so tight I almost choke.

After running out of my interview this morning, I called my financial advisor, and she helped me to clarify my ideas. Turns out, I'm not as poor as I thought—if I live in a place that's not crazy expensive, like Manhattan. Thank God I listened to my dad and made some good investments since getting my first paycheck, and I don't have to rely only on my checking account to go after my dream.

"You were the one telling me to grab my life by the balls and drag it where I wanted!" I choke a laugh.

She literally said that, and I can't hide the amusement in my voice. She's such a drama queen sometimes, but I love her anyway. My heart drums in my chest as if it wants to escape. This is the first time I'm



Wendy Ashford—The grump and the chef

leaving without knowing if and when I'll come back. I'll visit for sure, and she'll visit me, but the idea of not seeing her at least twice a week is something I don't know I'll ever get used to.

"Yes, but I meant something here in New York. I don't even know where you're going. Why aren't you telling me? Is there something wrong? Are you sick?" she whines, and my heart speeds up.

"I'm not sick, I swear! Don't even think that I would hide something like that from you." I try to reassure her, but I'm not sure I'm succeeding.

"So, why aren't you telling me?" She doesn't relent.

I know it's difficult for her to understand. We've shared the most intimate details of our lives since we've known each other. But this time, I need to find my dream before I can tell anyone about it. I'm not sure *where* exactly I'll find it. I can't just fly across the country for a man I don't know even know wants me, putting my dream on hold yet again. I've been doing that for too long, and I'm not happy with that. If fate brings me to Noah, I'll be beyond ecstatic, but I won't put myself last because of a man again. Noah has no intention of coming down from that mountain. He hasn't shown any interest in changing his ways or even compromising for me. And that scares me.

"I need to figure out if what I want to do is possible, and eventually, I'll call you, okay? I'll be fine. It's not like I'm disappearing." I chuckle, grabbing her shoulders and forcing her to look at me.

"Have you figured out what you want to do?" She sniffs, and I can see tears pooling in the corner of her eyes. I'll cry too if I stay any longer at this apartment instead of hailing a taxi.

"I think so. I always thought I couldn't afford to open a restaurant in New York. And it's true. But it's not like this is the only city in the world. Maybe I can make it work somewhere else." At least I have to try. There's a world out there waiting for me and my food.

"I'll miss you," she whispers in my ear, hugging me again.

"I'll miss you too." My voice cracks, and emotions clog my throat. I can't even swallow.

When I walk toward the taxi and help the guy put my suitcase in the trunk of his car, I don't look back. I know Ava's there, watching as I hop into the back seat and trying hard not to cry. I'm not sad. Terrified, sure, but in a good way. This is the first time I'm jumping into something I want instead of choosing the easy way, and it's so liberating I can hardly fathom it.

***

"Is this your first flight?" the old man asks when he notices my legs bouncing as I sit on the plane waiting for everyone to board the flight.

The wine I got at the airport bar did nothing to soothe my nerves. I thought at least ten times about turning around and walking straight out of the JFK terminal. But I always want to bolt when facing big life

Wendy Ashford—The grump and the chef

changes, especially if I don't have a detailed plan laid out in front of me, and this time I was prepared for it. I wasn't running this time.

"No. But I'm a bit nervous about what's waiting for me on the other side." I smile at him.

"Well, if it doesn't make you nervous, it's not worth it. Don't you think?"

I lower my gaze to my leg and put a sweaty palm on my jeans to stop the bouncing. I take a deep breath and look out the window, trying to empty my mind of the worry suffocating me.

I'm not sure if what this man says it's true, but I hope to find what I dream of when we land.

***

"Are you sure you want this one? It's been closed for a decade now. I have a more recent place in a town an hour from here," the real estate agent tells me. She obviously doubts I can make something useful out of this place.

I arrived from the airport just an hour ago, not even taking a shower before meeting her. Driving here in my rental car, I called the only real estate agency in town and asked if they had a commercial space available that could fit a restaurant. She was so eager to show me some places, I had the feeling I was her first phone call in a long time. The housing market is a bit slow during winter, but from the excitement in her voice, I don't think it's just a seasonal problem here.

"I'm sure this is the one. It needs some renovation, but I can work with that," I say, turning around and admiring the place.

It's an old diner with Formica tabletops and red vinyl benches lined against the windows. There's not much light in here, with the glass wall all boarded up, but I can see the potential. And the price is within the budget my financial advisor helped me figure out when I told her I was ready to jump into my new life. I'll probably need to do most of the work myself, but I don't think it will be a problem painting and cleaning this place. And I'll need a business plan, too, considering I'm jumping blindly into buying this property. It will be either the best decision of my life or the worst nightmare, but I'm following my guts. I can't contain the smile spreading over my face.

The realtor nods and smiles back, probably seeing the dreamy look in my eyes or maybe because she can finally get rid of a property that's been on her listings for a decade. "Okay, if you say you can do it, I trust you. Are you keeping it as a restaurant?"

Her hopeful tone makes me turn and study her face. She's in her mid-fifties, maybe, and she looks like she tried hard to impress me with the suit and heels. I bet she'll ditch both as soon as I sign the papers. She doesn't look comfortable in them, and I saw her fidgeting with her skirt a couple of times when she thought I wasn't looking. I feel a bit underdressed in my skinny



Wendy Ashford—The grump and the chef

jeans, loose hoodie, and messy hair from the almost eighteen-hour trip.

"A restaurant, yes. I want to keep it like this." The excitement bubbling inside me makes me rush my words.

She chuckles and seems almost relieved. "Thank God. We miss a good restaurant in this town. We have a pub, but there's nothing fancier than burgers and fries there."

It's a good start. At least I know she'll eat here sometimes. "I hope more people will think the same." I can't hide my nervousness.

"Trust me, we need a bit of life in this town. You don't see anyone around because there's nothing to do here. Sometimes, I want to go out with my family, but I give up when I think about having to drive an hour back and forth to eat pancakes or a steak. The previous owner closed down this place because he was old, not because the business was sinking," she reassures me, easing a bit of the weight off my chest.

"So, why did you want to show me the place an hour from here?" I chuckle.

"Because you're from New York! This isn't a fancy town with upscale shops and tourists. Jesus, the last time I put on a skirt was for my wedding thirty years ago," she confesses frankly.

I can't stop a laugh from coming out. "I don't want fancy and upscale. I want real and cozy," I whisper, turning around and taking in this place one last time.

If dreams can be made of dust and chipped paint,
I'm sure mine just came true.

# Chapter 23

"Are you okay in there?" A male voice reaches me from the other side of the stall door.

"Yeah, I think so." A raspy sound leaves my throat as I stand up, clean my mouth with toilet paper, and throw it in the toilet along with the contents of my stomach.

When I walk out, a man is washing his hands and looking at me in the mirror, smiling with pity.

"I fucking hate planes," I mumble before taking a sip from the faucet and rinsing my mouth.

He chuckles. "Yeah. Not a fan either. At least you resisted until you landed before throwing up. It's nasty for everyone sitting next to you when it happens on a plane."

"Lucky me." I try to smile too, but I fail.

I watch him fix his tie and walk out of the bathroom after waving goodbye. I stare at my reflection in the mirror and cringe. I'm a mess. What was I thinking



The grump and the chef—Wendy Ashford

when I asked Henry to lend me his truck and drove to the airport? Jumping on a plane without even an overnight bag is crazy. What do I do now? Show up at her place without showering or changing clothes?

I wash my face, comb my hair as best I can with my hands, and walk out of the bathroom. I walk into the first souvenir shop I see and buy a super expensive hoodie with the Brooklyn Bridge printed on it. It's hideous but better than the *"I love New York"* one. Right now, I hate New York. I haven't even left JFK and I already despise this place.

I change into my new attire and put my old clothes in the gift shop bag. My stomach is still a bit queasy, so I opt to skip the meal and go straight for a taxi. I swear, I've never seen so many people in the same place, but luckily, the line isn't too long, and I get into the back of a cab a few minutes later. The guy doesn't talk much, just munches on a bag of sunflower seeds all the way to our destination. I'm impressed at how fast he goes through the bag, and a bit disgusted when he spits the shells into another bag.

I look out the window, taking in the traffic surrounding us. I wonder how a sane person would willingly live in a place like this. It takes an eternity to reach Manhattan, and when we enter it, I'm immediately overwhelmed. So many people, cars, and noises, and I am terrified to drag my ass out of this taxi. The skyscrapers, though, are something I'll remember for-

Wendy Ashford—The grump and the chef

ever. It's strange; I should feel claustrophobic driving between these massive buildings, but I actually feel almost protected. It's a bit like being surrounded by the tall trees in Pinecreek. You can't see the sun peeking over the top there, either.

"We're here." The guy doesn't even turn around as he talks; just points to the building we're in front of through the rearview mirror.

I swipe my debit card to pay him and then step out of the car. He speeds away like he just dropped a bomb on the sidewalk.

I look up at the multi-story building covered in floor-to-ceiling mirrored windows and feel small. What the hell am I doing here? I lower my gaze to the people coming in and out of the front door, feeling like one of the homeless people I saw on the way here. Saying I'm underdressed is the understatement of the century. Every single person seems to be strolling right off of a runaway. I've never seen so many suits at once. What if I meet Olivia and she realizes she's ashamed of me? It's one thing to be holed up in my cabin where no one can see us together, but being here in the open, among *her* people, is a completely different story.

I take a deep breath and try to relax. It was a bad decision to jump on a plane and come here without a plan, but I *am* here right now, so I need to put on my big boy pants and walk through that door.

"Noah?" A feminine voice calling my name startles me.

I turn around and find a brunette staring at me like I'm an alien. I frown. "Do I know you?" I ask, but I'm sure I've never met her.

She smiles and shakes her head. "Not directly, but I called your phone a couple of times. I'm Ava."

The air leaves my lungs in a rush. What are the chances of meeting Olivia's best friend on a sidewalk in Manhattan? Well, I'm standing in front of her workplace, so the chances are better than zero.

"Nice to meet you! How do you know what I look like?" I'm more puzzled than ever.

She chuckles. "Olivia took lots of pictures of you, and trust me, you're not a guy someone can forget. And right now, you're standing out like a giraffe at the North Pole." She waves a hand in my direction, and I look down at my baggy jeans, boots, mountain jacket, and the freaking Brooklyn Bridge sweatshirt peeking out. I look like a lumberjack on the loose.

"Fair enough." I smile.

"What are you doing here?" she asks with a grin. She knows exactly why I'm here, and hope inflates in my chest. Maybe Olivia wants to see me, after all.

"I'm looking for Olivia," I explain.

"She doesn't work here anymore." She squints, studying me.

"I know. I hoped they'd give me a forwarding address for her apartment or something…" I wave at the door and realize I must sound like a fool. No company

228

would give out the address of a woman who doesn't even work for them anymore. Hell, if they did that, I'd personally punch them in the face.

"You didn't think through this, did you?" Her voice is tender, and she looks at me like I'm some sort of kid being overly dramatic.

"I…no. I just jumped on a plane without a plan in mind." I rub a hand over my face. "I know, it's stupid. I should just go home." I move to turn around and leave, but she grabs my arm and stops me.

"It's not stupid. It's sweet." She smiles at me. "But Olivia's not here. Not in New York," she explains.

I literally sway on my feet. "Where did she go?" I stutter.

She shakes her head, suddenly almost shy. "I don't know. She didn't tell me because she wanted to settle down before making the big announcement. I hear from her every day. She's okay, but I can't help you."

"Oh," is all I can think to say. My throat tightens, and my chest aches.

I've lost her. I was stupid to let her go without a fight, and now I have no chance of telling her that I love her. I was so sure I'd never see her again that I didn't even ask for her number. The irony is that I have Ava's number, and she doesn't know where her friend is. I bend down and put my hands on my knees. All this traveling and bad news are catching up with me.

Ava puts a hand on my back comfortingly. "Listen, I don't know right now, but as soon as she tells me, I'll call you, okay?" Her tone is reassuring but doesn't do much to ease the emptiness inside of me.

"Thank you," I whisper, standing up.

She's worried, and her deep frown tells me I don't look so good. I hope I don't pass out on this sidewalk. "What will you do now?" she asks.

I shake my head and try to clear my mind. "I don't know. I guess I'll go back to the airport and try to find a flight home."

She nods but says nothing as I turn around and look around like I can magically make a taxi appear in front of me.

"Let me help. I'll call an Uber to take you to the airport." I'm so confused by the news and the feelings crowding my chest that I just nod and let her take care of everything.

The car is nicer than the taxi that brought me here, but the trip to the airport is a blur. I feel like a fool for flying here, but also desperate to find her. She's the first good thing that's happened to me in ten years, and I was stupid to push her away. The reality is I made her feel unwelcome, and she jumped at the first chance she had to leave me. I let her believe I wanted to be alone, even though I was craving her presence in my cabin.

Wendy Ashford—The grump and the chef

The bell rings when I enter Henry's store, and he looks up from his phone. He takes in my appearance and makes a disgusted face.

"Don't say anything. I know. I haven't slept and showered since you last saw me," I explain as I put his truck keys on the counter in front of him.

"That was almost forty-eight hours ago!" He's trying to scold me, but it comes out sounding like worry.

"I know. It was stupid," I murmur, rubbing a hand over my face. "I'm going home, taking a shower, and sleeping for at least two days."

He nods and smiles. "Did you find her?" His tone makes me frown. It's like he's trying to hide a smirk.

"No. Can you at least pretend you're not enjoying my misery?" I don't like his smug expression. I've never seen it before on Henry's face. What am I missing?

"I thought so," is all he says.

"Why? What happened in the last forty-eight hours that I should know about?" I don't even know if I want an explanation. I'm tired, heartbroken, and starving. I don't want to play games.

"Nothing, but you might want to consider taking a look at the old diner." He beams.

I frown. The old diner's been closed since I was barely twenty. "What? Why?"

He shrugs his shoulders. "They say it was finally sold."

I'm too tired to understand what he's saying. Why should I care about an old, dusty restaurant that hasn't been open for years? I don't even care if they take it down and build a strip club.

"So what?" I'm pissed now.

"A New Yorker bought it," he states.

My brain is slow to catch up with his words, but when the realization reaches my foggy brain, I freeze. "Are you serious?" I whisper under my breath.

He just nods, and I bolt out of his store like it's on fire. I run a couple of doors down with my heart hammering in my chest. The diner is closed like it's always been, but the "Pending" sign under the "For Sale" one makes my chest squeeze. My brain can't keep up with what's happening when the door opens and a blond mop of hair peeks out.

Olivia looks up and smiles in my direction. All the air leaves my lungs, and I almost kneel on the sidewalk. She's here, and she is a vision I thought I wouldn't see again for the rest of my life.

I take a wobbly step toward her, then another, and when she spreads her arms and welcomes me, I hold her tight. I'm finally home.

Wendy Ashford—The grump and the chef

# Chapter 24

"What are you doing in town?" I ask Noah when he finally lets me go.

As soon as his body detaches from mine, I feel the cold emptiness that's been with me since I left the cabin.

Noah rubs a hand over the back of his neck and looks almost nervous. Now that I study him carefully, he looks tired, like he hasn't slept for days, and it worries me. I haven't had much sleep either in the last few days, but he seems on the verge of passing out or falling asleep on the sidewalk.

"Honestly, I just came from New York," he confesses.

My eyes snap to his, trying to understand if he's telling the truth. He never leaves his cabin, but he just casually visits a city on the other coast? "Are you serious? Why did you go to New York?" My brain is so overwhelmed by questions I can hardly get the words out.

He chuckles and rubs his eyes with a couple of fingers. "I was looking for you. I went to your former office, and Ava was there. She told me you'd left town. So, I went back to the airport and came home," he explains in a rush as my mouth hangs open.

I can't process what he just said. This is Noah, the hermit who lives in a cabin buried in the snow. He's never left this county, and now he's telling me he traveled across the entire country?

"You flew to New York, and when you couldn't find me, you flew back here? No resting in between?" I ask, baffled.

He shakes his head. "About forty-eight hours, round trip. I can't even stand up right now," he confesses.

"Sweet Jesus," I whisper. "Why would you do that?"

He smiles and buries his hands in his front pockets. "Because I love you, and I wanted to tell you."

My heart hammers in my chest. This is the most romantic, crazy thing anyone's ever done for me. And I thought he wanted nothing to do with me! When I came back here, I thought I'd have to wait until spring to see him again. And that I'd have to work hard to make him fall in love with me. I close the distance between us and hug him tightly. His arms envelop my body, reciprocating my gesture.

"I love you too. And I bought an old restaurant to show you how much I love you. And I'll probably end up broke and poor, but I don't care," I mumble with my

Wendy Ashford—The grump and the chef

face pressed into the warm jacket that smells like him. I've missed his scent. I've missed his body against mine. I've missed him.

Noah chuckles again and tightens his grip. "Are we competing for the craziest romantic gesture? Because if we are, you win, hands down."

I giggle and tilt my head back to look into his eyes. "I wanted to follow my dream, and Pinecreek has what I need to make it come true. You happen to live here, and I'm not complaining about that. You're the cherry on top. A big, sexy cherry."

He laughs and lowers to kiss my lips. I've missed his kisses. I tiptoe and press my mouth on his. I kiss him slowly as his hands cradle my face in a sweet, caring embrace. He slips his tongue between my lips, and I savor this moment that tastes more like love than the lust that consumed us over the past weeks.

"So, are you going to show me your restaurant?" he whispers against my mouth.

I smile and nod. "We haven't finalized the contract yet, but they're letting me take a look inside to make a list of what needs fixing. They say the signature is a mere formality at this point."

I drag him through the door, and my heart starts beating faster. This will be my diner, my dream, and he wants me to show him around. I watch Noah's smile as he takes in the old furniture and the dusty countertop. He seems almost proud of this mess.

"There's a lot to do," I rush to explain, "but I can fix most of it myself. I need to call someone to assess if the kitchen needs repairing or if everything is working. It's been closed for ten years, so I expect a lot of work will be needed in that area."

Suddenly, I feel unsure of my decision. What if Noah thinks I'm crazy for making an offer on this place? It's falling apart, for Pete's sake!

"I like it. I forgot what it looked like inside." He looks back at me. "I can take a look at the kitchen if you want. I can help you," he proposes hesitantly.

I'm surprised. "Really? I don't want to inconvenience you. I mean, I'll pay you, of course!"

He puts a hand around my shoulder and drags me to him. "I wasn't asking for a job. I just want to help you. It's what a boyfriend is supposed to do. It's my duty." He grins and searches my face for a reaction.

That boyfriend part wasn't a slip-up. It was intentional. I can see it in the sincerity of his eyes. A warmth expands in my chest when my heart understands what he's actually offering.

"So, you're applying for a boyfriend job, huh? A position has opened up recently. Please leave your resumé on the counter, and I'll let you know when to come in for an interview." I cross my arms on my chest and fight back a laugh.

Noah smirks and licks his lower lip. God, I would like to lick every single inch of his glorious body. "A

236

resumé? I thought I already went through an extensive interview process back at my cabin. What was it that didn't convince you? My oral skills? A lack in the package department?"

He corners me against the counter, and I feel the heat pooling between my legs. Jesus. I'm already wet for him. "Oh, no, the package is fine. More than adequate. The oral skills, now, I might need a repeat of that. Just to be sure," I say coyly, and his eyes darken with lust.

He grabs me by the waist and, in a swift move, sits me on the counter. I squeal in surprise. I can't get over the fact that he can handle me like a rag doll despite my weight. Without a word, he slips a couple of fingers under the waistband of my leggings and drags them down with my panties.

I inhale sharply when he kisses me and then bends over, licking his way to my clit and sucking on it hard. I moan and slip my fingers into his air, enjoying the intense pleasure running freely through my body. And just like that, with Noah going down on me on the counter of my diner, I realize it's not so scary jumping blindly into your dream—if you have someone holding your hand and jumping with you.

# Epilogue

*Two years later*

I finish harvesting the last of the tomatoes and put them into the crate. The cart is full of our summer vegetables, and I push it across our property and exit from the back gate. It's a short walk to the diner, and when I pass in front of Henry's store, he runs out to stop me.

"What do you have here? Can I take a look?" he asks, almost tripping over the cart.

"Sure, but I can't guarantee you'll find what you want when I come back. You know Olivia has the first choice of the vegetables."

Since she opened the diner a year and a half ago, we've started growing our own produce and using it in most of the recipes she comes up with. Sometimes, we have too many vegetables for her to use in the kitchen, and I give them to Henry to sell in his store. Other times, we go to the farmers market to buy what we don't grow in our backyard.



Wendy Ashford—The grump and the chef

"The zucchinis you gave me last week were gone by noon. I had to break up a fight between Sam and Thomas over the last one," he explains, as though to convince me to give him more than last time.

I chuckle. Since coming down from that mountain two years ago, Olivia and I have become *the* talk of this town. We're the king and queen of their world or at least their meals. The truth is, we brought some life into this place. Not bad for someone everyone considered an unapproachable grump.

Olivia opened *The Twist*—her traditional diner with a twist—six months after she bought it, and the place is flourishing. Ava came to visit with a friend from New York for the opening. Turns out, her friend is a famous travel and food blogger who posted about Olivia's restaurant on her website, and since then, this place has been packed, especially during the summer. Somehow Pinecreek has entered tourists' radars, partly because this place is perfect for hiking and outdoor activities and partly because every travel or food blogger in the country wants to visit the restaurant. The good reviews skyrocketed, and locals are not complaining, especially since there is more money coming into town. Every business in town has benefitted from it.

We went from having zero lodging options to two bed and breakfasts in town. One of them is our home. The house behind the church that Tom was selling was too small, but we were able to expand Olivia's mother's cabin. Now we have a five-bedroom place, where we rent three of the bedrooms and live in the other two. I take care of the bed and breakfast, and Olivia the diner.

"I'll see what I can do, but no promises. She gets feral when she sees perfect tomatoes." I laugh, and Henry does too.

I've discovered that Olivia is a perfectionist in the kitchen. She doesn't have a set menu. She chooses what to cook based on what she can find at the farmers market that day. She won't buy produce that isn't fresh just because the dish is on the menu. She says a chef has to adapt to what nature offers, not the other way around, and I agree. I've never tasted food so good in my entire life. What she made for us in the cabin during our first winter together was just a tiny glimpse of her full potential.

"God, sometimes she scares me. When she starts grilling the farmers about what they feed their livestock or whether the eggs are genuinely from free-range chickens, I feel sorry for them." He shudders, and I know what he means. Sometimes, she scares me too.

I pat him on the shoulder as he turns around and walks back inside. I push my cart to the back entrance where the kitchen is and push it open. Sarah comes to help me to load the crates inside.

"What are you doing here? Shouldn't you be resting at home?" I ask Olivia when I spot her in front of the stove.

She turns around with a smile. I'll never get used to the flutter in my chest when she looks at me like I'm her entire world. Only with Olivia have I realized what it means to be truly in love. I've never been as happy as I am right now.

"I'm just checking the sauce, I promise!" She wobbles toward the back entrance.

"You are super pregnant. Due in a week. Why aren't you sitting down and resting? That's what we hired Sarah for!" I plead, for the umpteenth time in the last couple of months.

Every time I turn my back, she's sneaking out to come here. "You won't let me do anything at home. I'm bored out of my mind!" she protests, pouting.

Sarah chuckles as she checks the produce and picks out what she needs for the diner. "I tried to kick her out, but she's a round stubborn thing!" She winks at Olivia.

I kneel in front of Olivia and kiss her huge belly. She's gained a bit of weight in the last couple of months, her belly expanded like a balloon, her legs swollen, and she has never been so beautiful. I didn't understand why they say pregnant women "glow" until I saw Olivia carrying our first child. She is beyond gorgeous. And her glorious boobs are huge—a perk I'm not complaining about at all.

"Can you please not give birth to our kid in this kitchen?" I ask, looking up at her.

She reaches out and caresses my face. "Only if you promise to rub my feet. It's been two months since I saw them, and I'm pretty sure they're exploding. I can feel it."

Looking down, I chuckle. "You do realize your flip-flops don't match, right?"

She gasps. "Really? That's why they feel different!" She tries to bend down to look but gives up when she almost topples over.

I stand up and grab her hand. "Come with me. I'll rub your feet and your back too." I drag her out and turn around to thank Sarah.

She reassures me, saying, "Don't worry about the veggies. I'll give Henry whatever we don't need. Go home and take care of her."

"Thank Sarah!" Olivia waves at her.

We stroll home, Olivia gripping my hand tightly as she wobbles next to me. We take our time, enjoying the summer sun kissing our skin. I look at Olivia and feel my chest expand with happiness and serenity.

In my early twenties, I thought my life would be nothing but misery. I never imagined that ten years later, a five-foot-tall, chatty blonde would barge into my life in the middle of a storm and show me what real happiness is.

Wendy Ashford—The grump and the chef

# About Wendy Ashford

Wendy Ashford loves to write spicy small-town romance novels that end with a Happily Ever After. She lives in the Pacific Northwest with her husband, dog, and cat. She loves the beach during winter and walking in the snow.

She likes to read, play with Legos, and watch romantic comedies on Netflix when not writing.

Follow her on social media:

Facebook: https://www.facebook.com/wendyashfordbooks

Instagram: https://www.instagram.com/author_wendy_ashford/

Newsletter: https://wendyashford.com/newsletter/

# Acknowledgments

In the ups and downs of my writing journey, I have been lucky to be surrounded by support and inspiration. To the grumps, whose quips and quirks light up the moments of solitude, you are my treasured companions on this literary voyage.

Your skepticism challenged my ideas, your cynicism offered perspective, and your witty banter infused laughter into the challenge of writing an entire book. In your grumpiness lay an unspoken encouragement, pushing me to refine, rethink, and rework until the words found their resonance.

To all the grumps out there, thank you for being the unexpected muse, the friendly critics, and the steadfast allies in this writer's odyssey. Your presence, though often cloaked in dissent, has added an irreplaceable depth to this novel. You are, without doubt, my favorite companions.

With heartfelt gratitude,

Wendy Ashford

www.ingramcontent.com/pod-product-compliance
Lightning Source LLC
Chambersburg PA
CBHW021428150726
47989CB00001B/160